THE ALCHEMYST'S MIRROR

LIZ DELTON

The Alchemyst's Mirror
Liz Delton

ISBN 978-1-7345231-5-7
Library of Congress Control Number: 2020918079
Copyright © 2020 Liz Delton

Tourmaline & Quartz Publishing
P. O. Box 193, North Granby, CT 06060
www.TourmalineandQuartzPublishing.com

One

PETRA

It was a fine night for spying. Bright moonlight flickered off the small quartz oval as Petra Everturn removed it from the print shop window. She slipped it into the pocket of her burgundy overcoat and strode away, clutching the rare—and somewhat illegal—Talmanian quartz she had placed there earlier. It would soon tell her everything she needed to know. Her black boots made almost no noise on the cobblestones as she quickly made her way back to the tea shop down the empty lane.

She headed down another street and turned onto Cordial Crescent, where Everturn's Finest Tea Shoppe stood amid the glowing evening streetlights.

As she reached for her big brass door key in another coat pocket, she heard the slightest sound behind her. Hands grabbed both her arms before she could turn around.

"What's that in your pocket?" a gruff voice asked.

"What's *what* in what pocket?" she grumbled, trying to shrug out of the man's grip.

He scoffed. "Let's try a different route. Why are you spying on the print shop?"

Petra bristled. "Unhand me at once."

Much to Petra's surprise, he did, but then he spun her around to face him. A pistol was aimed at her middle, deftly held in the shadow of his coat. She looked up from the pistol into a scruffy face: weathered and bearded. He looked only a little older than her twenty years, but the beard made him seem much older. She would have taken him for a vagrant had it not been for the tailored suit and coat. Respectable men in Harrowdel did not have beards.

She crossed her arms over her chest. "What do you want?" She slipped one hand inside her coat under cover of her crossed arms, trying to reach her own pistol without him noticing.

He grinned behind the beard.

Just a little further. Her fingers brushed the tip of her pistol's handle.

"Me?" he asked, still grinning at her. "I want—" he reached out and yanked her hand away, lunging for the pistol holstered under her arm "—to know why you're spying on the printer."

"I don't—" she began.

"Enough pretense," he snapped, pointing both guns at her. "I saw you plant the crystal earlier, and I know what it does. Tell me now, or your sister will be running your little tea shop all by herself come morning."

Petra clenched her fists. So, he not only knew how the Talmanian quartz worked, but who she was, too.

"Fine. Fine. But not here." She glanced up and down Cordial Crescent. "I don't think either of us wants the magistrate's night guards joining our conversation, do we?"

He narrowed his eyes at her. "Very well."

"And you're going to give me my pistol back," she said.

He laughed, twirling her pistol around his finger but still pointing his own at her. "And why would I want to do that?"

"Well," said a sweet voice from behind him, "it depends on how much you want to live." Petra's younger sister Maisie stepped out from the shadowed alley behind the man, holding a shotgun.

Petra grinned and grabbed both pistols out of the man's hands.

Maisie was the opposite of Petra in almost every way. Where Petra was tall and more imposing than most men, Maisie was short and nearly always smiling. Petra had long, black hair, and Maisie's was curly and golden. They both had golden eyes just like their father, which was the only trait they shared. And neither of them was defenseless.

"I think we should still talk," Petra said, jabbing one of the pistols in the man's back and pushing him toward the door of the tea shop.

Maisie unlocked the door and drew the curtains once they were all inside. It was dark inside the shop, but Petra could see by the streetlight filtering in through the semi-translucent curtains. Cordial Crescent was in a well-lit section of Harrowdel's merchant quarter, on the first of the city's six levels. Each level rose up like enormous steps coming up from the port, and they were connected by lifts running up each plateau's façade. The lifts down here on the First Rise were practical: massive steam-powered elevators that were big enough to transport entire carriages with horses between rises. As you went up to the higher rises, the lifts reflected the people who patronized them: too clean, frilly, and extravagant. That's how Petra always thought of them, anyway.

Maisie bustled to the back of the shop, no doubt off to check on something in the oven. Petra caught a whiff of burnt pastry. She was just glad Maisie had come outside to check on her.

The man who had accosted her stood awkwardly by the door, his hands clasped in front of him, and his gaze alternating between the pistols in Petra's hands, and the interior of the shop. He looked almost innocent standing there, as if he could be one of her brother's friends caught in an act of wrong-doing.

In addition to his well-tailored suit and jacket, his fashionable shoes were highly polished, and upon closer inspection, his flaxen hair and beard were at least neat and trimmed evenly. The chain of a watch dangled from his vest pocket, and he had a bronze-set emerald pierced through his ear. He was definitely not from Harrowdel.

"Well? Who are you?" Petra asked, pushing him into a

nearby chair. Even if he looked innocent now, he had been threatening her only minutes ago.

He grabbed hold of the small spindly table for balance. She brandished both pistols at him, inviting him to speak.

"Evan Rosslyn, at your service." He mimed tipping a nonexistent hat.

"What do you want?"

"Exactly what I asked you before," he said. "To know why you're using a Talmanian quartz to spy on the printer."

"It's none of your business," Petra said.

Maisie returned, having exchanged her shotgun for a tea tray. Petra suppressed a grin. Maisie was ever the helpful one.

"Do you work for the printer?" Maisie asked, setting the tea tray down on the table and brushing floury hands on her rose-colored skirt. She sat, ignoring Petra's warning look, and poured three cups of tea from the gold and white teapot, steam rising between them all like the curl of a question mark.

Petra kept both pistols leveled at the man.

"What? No, I don't work for them." He eyed the tea suspiciously.

Maisie took a deep drink out of her own cup. "Then why do you care if we were spying on him?"

After seeing Maisie drink the tea, Evan reached out and lifted his own cup to his lips, tasting it. Their shop was famous for its tea, after all. "Because I want to hire you."

Petra laughed. "Hire us? To cater your wedding, or

serve a private afternoon tea, you mean?"

He chuckled, but his fingers were clenched tight around the teacup's handle. "Where did you get the crystal, anyway?"

Petra handed Maisie his gun and grabbed a biscuit from the tea tray. "How do you know what it is?" she countered.

"I travel," he said, and gave a little cough. He drank some more tea, and said, "Well? Will you work for me? I think your skills suit the project. You would be compensated. And of course, if you do accept, I won't report to the magistrate that the Everturns are in possession of a highly illegal Talmanian quartz."

Maisie frowned. "That's blackmail."

"That's life," he said. He took another sip of tea and coughed again. This time, it was a deep, throaty cough, and he spat something into his hand.

"And that's poison," Maisie said.

He put the teacup back on its saucer slowly, staring at Maisie with his mouth open. Petra grinned. Maisie was ever the helpful one.

"What do you really want with us?" Petra asked.

"Perhaps I can find the antidote to the poison I wiped on the inside of your teacup before it really takes effect," Maisie said, sipping her own tea carelessly. "If you tell us."

He gaped at her.

"Truly," his voice was panicked now. "I just wished to hire you. I saw you plant the quartz this morning, and I followed you back to your shop to find out who you were." He coughed again.

Petra threw an embroidered napkin at him. "We are not spies."

Evan coughed into the napkin and doubled over, hacking.

"Promise you'll back off?" Maisie asked. She tapped him on the shoulder, and he looked up to see her holding a small glass bottle.

He nodded fervently, unable to stop coughing. She handed him the bottle, and he guzzled it.

Petra and Maisie shared a look as Evan coughed a few more times, then subsided.

Petra fingered the stone in her pocket. "Get out," she told him. She was anxious to see what answers the quartz held for her.

"But—"

The girls hefted their pistols again.

"I really think we can help each other—"

"Don't care," Petra said, lifting him by his jacket collar then steering him toward the door. "We don't want to see you here ever again."

The bell over the shop door tinkled merrily as she shoved him into the street.

Maisie waved his pistol in the air. "And I'm keeping this. It's pretty."

Bewilderment, scorn, and disappointment fought for prevalence on his face as they slammed the door shut and bolted it. Maisie turned her back to it and laughed.

Petra shook her head and strode to the back of the

shop, tucking her pistol back in its holster. Maisie was the only person she knew who would laugh in a situation like this.

"Well that was fun," her sister said, following her into the kitchen at the back of the shop. The homey room was lit only by an old-style fireplace across from the bank of three ovens that normally kept the room at a high temperature. Their cat Biscuit lounged near the fireplace, eyes closed but his tail swishing around him. Evidence of Maisie's recent baking was strewn everywhere—dough set to rise on the back of the counter, piping hot scones cooling on a tray in the corner, and a dozen or so petit fours on a baking sheet, half of them glazed, next to an assortment of bowls filled with different colors of confection waiting to cover them.

Petra snorted, eyeing the petit fours. "Where did you get poison?"

"Oh, it wasn't poison," Maisie said, double-checking that her ovens were off. "A few months ago, we accidentally ordered Abysmal Cherry root instead of Artisanal Cherry—it just causes rapid swelling and coughing. Marshmallow leaf clears it right up." She took the glass bottle of 'antidote' from her dress pocket and put it on the counter.

Petra laughed. "Nice trick."

"So, did you get it?" Maisie said, her tone growing serious.

In answer, Petra pulled the crystal from her pocket and held it up to shine in the firelight.

Maisie bit her bottom lip. "Do you think the printer really knows anything about Jiordan's disappearance?"

"We're about to find out," Petra said, pulling a small device from the leather holster hanging at her hip. She had built it from a diagram they found in their father's workshop in the basement, the same place they had gotten the crystal. "But Maisie, don't be disappointed if it's nothing. We have other leads."

Maisie looked away and grabbed a bowl of glaze for the petit fours and began stirring it. The top layer of hardened sugar dissolved back into the mix. "I know. Let's just watch it."

Petra pressed the quartz oval into the waiting tines of the device with a snap. As soon as she did, light sprang up from the device, shining through the Talmanian quartz and projecting a moving image of the print shop in the air above the work table.

Maisie had called it magic when they first tested it. Petra knew the mechanics behind the projecting device since she had built it, but had no idea why the crystal, when exposed to light shone through an opposing piece of black quartz, could replay images it had been exposed to, and sounds to some extent. She decided it was only half magic, but only until she could find out the science behind it.

Petra and Maisie watched in rapt attention as the projection showed them the day at the print shop in amorphous scenes, listening for any mention of their brother, Jiordan Everturn.

The Harrowdel Gazette had reported last week that Jiordan, a well-known adventurer and explorer, had met his end in the mountains of Pruvia. It had been disturbingly similar to the time when Petra was eleven and found out about her parents' deaths while they were on an expedition in Scitica. Jiordan, sixteen at the time, had taken over the tea shop from their parents, until about five years later when he too decided Harrowdel wasn't big enough for him, and began exploring just like their father.

He had been missing for months now, maybe longer. After the article was printed, Petra questioned the man who ran the Gazette, but he had told her he couldn't reveal his source for privacy reasons. And she couldn't threaten a fellow merchant with a pistol unless she wanted to be thrown in the magistrate's dungeon for a while.

They watched the projected recording for hours, Petra's hopes diminishing. Maisie's normally cheerful expression turned inward, and she grabbed another bowl of icing to finish decorating the petit fours.

Finally, they watched the printer close up the shop and leave, and Petra unclipped the crystal from the device. The projection disappeared, leaving only disappointment in the air.

Maisie continued to ice the petit fours, adding unnecessary details to the frosted designs already decorating the little cakes.

"I'm sorry," Petra said after several minutes of silence. "But it was just one lead. That idiot probably just made it up, like I've been telling you."

"You're probably right," Maisie said, putting down a bag of purple icing.

Petra reached out and grabbed one of the cakes with purple flowers on it before Maisie could protest. Petra couldn't bake if her life depended on it, but Maisie had been baking for the tea shop since before they had become its sole caretakers. Their father opened the shop after his first big expedition brought him fame and fortune. It had always been a dream of their mother's. After they died, Jiordan took over, while Petra helped serve tea until she was old enough to help with the books. Maisie was always underfoot in the kitchen until their old baker realized Maisie had a talent for pastries.

The shop was filled with artifacts from their father's expeditions, and a few of Jiordan's, too. In the main part of the shop, an enormous woven tapestry depicting the Scitican harvest rites in rich purple and green hues hung above the marble fireplace; next to it, a large glass sphere on a stand which their father claimed was how a certain Pruvian tribe would tell weather; various timepieces littered the shop, the largest an enormous brass clock from Rancozzi; and their mother's collection of tea paraphernalia interspersed between the artifacts like bits of confection on a buffet table. Jiordan's collection was sparse compared to their father's. Of course, their father had been an adventurer for much longer, and Jiordan had only a few years' experience.

Petra gasped as the clink of a teacup hitting the floor sounded, and she saw their cat dart from the kitchen.

"Biscuit!" she hissed. "Get back here!"

Maisie snorted. "It's not like he's going to help clean it up." She went over beside the counter to crouch down over the teacup. "It's only chipped. It's not one of the good ones anyway."

Petra rolled her eyes at the departed cat and grabbed a rag, bending down to help Maisie clean up the spilled tea.

What had happened to Jiordan? Petra wondered as she sopped up the tea. Despite what she had said to Maisie, she was worried. She remembered all too well the awful truth when her parents had died. Maisie, only three years younger than Petra, had been eight at the time.

But they had to find out for sure what happened to their brother, and she was running out of options. There were no other leads. Only half-baked ideas and half-true tales.

"There's someone out front with a delivery, Miss Everturn," Khalia, one of their serving girls said, poking her head into the storage room where Petra was checking the tea inventory an hour before the shop opened.

"Tell them to go to the back," Petra said, marking down a number in her ledger. She straightened her burgundy coat and brushed the tea dust off her black trousers before heading to the delivery hatch at the back of the shop.

A man stood with his back to her, a large trunk propped against the doorframe. He turned and recognized the beard and emerald stud immediately. She reached for her pistol but kept it in its holster—at this time of day, the alley was populated with several other shopkeepers and delivery boys.

"You!" she said.

Evan Rosslyn grimaced, and ran his hand once over his beard. "Yes, me. Now before you try to poison me again, I've a valid reason for being here this time. I think you should hear me out."

"What," she said through gritted teeth. She wished Maisie were here, but she had gone to the market for fresh blueberries for some turnovers she was making.

Evan poked the trunk beside him with his polished shoe, his face flushed red with excitement. "It came off the ship I just sailed in on from Amaryllia. They found it when they were unloading the cargo this morning. The instructions say, 'Deliver to Misses Maisie and Petra Everturn, Cordial Crescent, Harrowdel in Adonia, upon my death. Signed, Jiordan W. Everturn.'"

Two

MAISIE

"Well, aren't you going to open it?" Evan asked, drumming his fingers on the counter he leaned against.

After Maisie had returned from the market clutching a small sack of expensive out of season blueberries, she had found Petra yelling at Evan in the back alley. When Maisie realized the trunk's significance, she directed Evan to bring it inside. She had mechanically poured tea for everyone while they all stared at the trunk. Petra had told Khalia to go home; they wouldn't open the shop today, and would have to cancel several reservations.

"No," Maisie whispered.

Evan stopped drumming his fingers.

"No. He can't be dead. This is all wrong."

With shaking hands, Maisie took a sip from her tea. It was Rose Oolong tea, her favorite. She couldn't taste it.

In a detached way, she noticed Evan ignoring his tea completely. She had a strange urge to laugh, until her gaze landed on the trunk again. She pressed herself against the counter for support.

Petra sat at the work table in front of a plate of petit fours. She had eaten five since coming into the kitchen with Evan and the trunk. Maisie didn't care. They were for Mistress Walliope's weekly Wednesday luncheon, which they had cancelled. She would have to make fresh ones anyway, since Mistress Walliope could tell if her pastries were more than a day old.

"Look," Evan said. "I'm sorry about last night. Truly." He absently pushed his teacup further away on the counter. "But when I found out who you were, well, it was too much of a coincidence. I should have explained myself better last night. And then when they found the trunk amid the cargo, well, I just had to take the chance and return."

Maisie watched Petra roll her eyes and take another petit four.

Without any argument from the girls, Evan continued. "In fact, it turns out I was looking for you two in the first place. I came to Adonia looking for Jiordan."

Petra looked up sharply. "What do you want with him?"

"So you don't think he's dead?" Maisie asked.

"Not at all."

"What do you want with him?" Petra repeated slowly.

Evan smoothed his beard. "Well, you see, I'm looking for this artifact. It's... highly valuable and potentially dangerous. I know Jiordan was searching for it in

Amaryllia, too, before he disappeared. I've been trying to track him down for ages. One of my sources suggested he could have gone home to Harrowdel, so I sailed here. It was my last lead on him."

He looked hopefully at the trunk.

"No," Petra said, noting his gaze. "We're not opening it yet. That note... It just doesn't feel right. You can drink your tea and leave." One corner of her mouth rose in a smirk.

Maisie bit her lip. "What was this artifact you were both searching for?"

He hesitated. "There have been rumors of it circulating for decades, but the respectable scholars always said it was just a myth. A seemingly magical artifact spoken of in both Adonian and Amaryllian tales that points to sorcerers, metallurgists and even—" he lowered his voice, "an underground alchemyst society."

"Yes, but what is it?" Petra asked, irritated.

"Oh, right. Well, it's called the Alchemyst's Mirror."

"What does this have to do with our brother?" said Maisie.

"I met Jiordan in Pruvia last year, and we happened to sail to Amaryllia on the same ship. I learned that he was also pursuing the Mirror. We even discussed some of our findings together."

"How do we know you didn't just kill him and come here to get the trunk?" Petra said. Maisie drew a sharp breath, staring between the two of them.

Evan frowned, and placed a hand to his chest as though

wounded. "How dare you suggest such a thing? Jiordan and I were—well, not quite *friends*, but amicable rivals at the very least. Besides, I brought it over here for you, didn't I?"

Maisie reached into her deep skirt pocket and put a hand on the pistol she had tucked in there this morning—Evan's pistol from last night. Petra was less subtle. She pulled out a knife from one of the many pockets of her overcoat.

"What is this Mirror thing you're looking for anyway? What does it do?" Maisie asked.

Evan kept his gaze on Petra's knife, which she began balancing point first on the worn work table, and spinning in circles. "Well, the name comes from this text written over four hundred years ago—" Petra lifted her knife and made a *get on with it* gesture. "—It's rumored to contain each of the seven metals of alchemy, an impossible feat of metallurgy to say the least. And each corresponds to one of what used to be thought of as the seven planets. It's said it can transport the person holding it to another place."

The Everturns were silent as his words sunk in.

"Transport? What do you mean?" Maisie asked.

"I mean, it's said to *send*, or move the user to another place of their imagining, without them taking a step or boarding a ship and so on. Like that," he snapped his fingers. "Ludicrous as it might sound, I've been looking for the Mirror for over two years now, since I first heard about it. It's an explorer's dream, really. One could travel the world in an instant, and not waste months aboard ships, or trekking through jungle."

"You don't really believe—" Petra began.

"Why not?" Evan said. "You can't tell me, living here—with all of these artifacts of your father's—that you don't believe *a little*. How do you think the Talmanian quartz works? Hmm?"

Petra sputtered. "Well that's—it's clearly—there's science we just don't understand yet."

Evan smiled. "Exactly. It's just science we don't understand yet. That's one way of looking at it."

"So our brother was looking for this Alchemyst's Mirror too?" Maisie asked.

He nodded, leaning back against the counter. "We parted ways when we arrived at the Port of Cerise in Amaryllia, but we would meet every month or so for a drink and to discuss our searches, compare our findings. Three months ago, I came calling at the tavern he'd been lodging at, but the tavern keeper said the rooms were empty. No one had seen him. I've been trying to find him since. At first, because I thought he had discovered something about the whereabouts of the Mirror, but then when I found not a scratch of a clue, I wondered if something had happened to him."

Maisie looked down at the trunk. How could her brother arrange for its delivery if he were dead? Yet, why would it have arrived here with that note if he weren't? She gnawed on her bottom lip.

"That tea's not poisoned, you know," she finally said

to Evan.

His mouth quirked into a smile, and he lifted one shoulder in half a shrug. "Well, it's cold now anyway."

She reached over and tossed it into the sink, then poured him some fresh tea from the pot kept warm on a glass trivet over a candle.

"So, are you going to open it?" he asked again. He took a tentative sip of the tea as if to show them he wasn't afraid.

"No," she and Petra said in unison. They looked at each other and smiled a little.

"Not right now," Petra added. "I want to find out more about what he was doing, and how that trunk even got here. I don't like it just showing up with that note saying—saying what it said."

Evan slipped his hands into his coat pockets. "Very well. But I'm not giving up on you two." He took another sip of tea, having found himself not poisoned from the first. "I've got lodgings at the Boxton Inn down on the Low Rise. Come find me there when you change your minds."

He pulled a small card from his pocket and placed it on the table before draining his cup and walking out.

Maisie couldn't get the trunk open. Petra had gone to the banker's after a quiet morning in the closed shop, and an even quieter lunch together, so Maisie had snuck upstairs to their shared attic bedroom where they had brought it. Even after Evan had left, Petra still didn't want to open the trunk, and Maisie wasn't sure why.

She was dying to find out what Jiordan had sent them—it must be full of clues to his whereabouts. She didn't believe he was dead. The note was wrong.

But she couldn't get the thing open. There was no latch that she could identify, nor anywhere to even stick a key.

She huffed, then kneeled on the braided rug covering the attic bedroom floor and began to examine the trunk closer. She ran her hands along the edges, her fingers bumping over the brass rivets embedded in the leather. The seam where the lid met the bottom was so tight that she couldn't even wedge a fingernail into it, let alone the screwdriver she had brought up from her father's workshop.

A strange scene was depicted on the carved wooden lid, painted with rudimentary strokes. It looked like some bizarre children's book drawing. In the top corner, a raven with its beak open surveyed the scene. In the center, there was a pool of water, with strange symbols carved all around it. A strange blue lion caught her eye, standing beside a phoenix, and a peacock hiding partially behind a tree.

The attic door eased open, and Maisie grabbed the screwdriver off the lid just in time and stuffed it in her skirt pocket. Petra looked surprised to see her there. She shucked off her knee-length coat with its many pockets and hung it neatly on the peg by her bed.

"What are you doing up here?" Petra asked. "Weren't you going to start those cakes for dowager Prowley's rescheduled tea?" She loosened her pistol holster as she sat down on the backless bench at the end of her bed and removed her tall leather boots to rub her feet. The bench had been their mother's, with golden button tufts, and rolled armrests covered in red velvet.

"I just came up to change my dress," Maisie said. "I got custard all over this one." It was true, but normally she didn't really care when she had a full day of baking ahead of her. "The cakes are cooling now."

She ducked behind the folding panels that hid her side of the attic. She only had the panels up because Petra couldn't stand the way Maisie kept her side of the attic, and Maisie couldn't stand Petra's remarks about keeping it clean. Dresses, skirts, petticoats, and stockings were strewn across the floor and hanging off her chaise lounge. Every inch of her vanity table held jars and tins of cosmetics, perfumes, or hair oils, and brushes and bows spilled from the drawer. Her window that looked out onto Cordial Crescent held all manner of candles, trinkets, and dried flowers on the sill. She slid the screwdriver out of her pocket and placed it quietly on the vanity.

"I just got distracted by that image on top of the trunk. It's so strange. Any idea what it is?" Maisie had tried to talk to Petra about the trunk over lunch, but her sister had been tight-lipped. She didn't know why Petra would ignore such an obvious new lead. The note was troubling, of course, but Maisie didn't believe it—couldn't believe it.

She rifled through a pile of clothes she knew to be mostly clean and selected a cherry-colored dress with white lace trim. Their cat Biscuit darted out from under her bed and ran around her panels, no doubt to go nap under Petra's bed instead.

"No idea," Petra said.

"Come on," Maisie prodded, tossing her dirty gown into the pile near her hamper. "Why don't you want to open it?" She stared at her pink and mauve folding screens as if she could see Petra through them.

Petra sighed. "I didn't know Jiordan could even carve wood."

"How do you know he carved it?" Maisie asked, glad Petra was at least talking about it.

"His initials are carved in the corner; it looks like the same hand that did the rest."

"Really?" Maisie asked, coming out from behind her folding panels and smoothing the sides of the cherry dress. She kneeled back down in front of the trunk and ran her fingers over the initials. "J.W.E., and what's that, a little star?"

A seven-pointed star made up the period after the 'E'. Petra shrugged, then went back to the bench at the end of her bed to rub her feet again.

"So, when do you think we should...?" Maisie ran a finger over the pond carved onto the trunk.

"Open it? You tried already didn't you?"

Maisie snorted, then shrugged. "Yep, wouldn't budge,

though. Let's open it now, come on Petra. This is a way better lead than the print shop."

Petra huffed. "I don't want to open it yet."

"Is it because of the note?"

"No," Petra hedged. "I just don't like the idea of this trunk falling into our laps after all of our searching. It doesn't seem like something he'd do. Who knows if it's really from Jiordan? What do all those symbols mean? I just don't want to be surprised."

"But how will we find out any answers unless we open it?" Maisie argued, her hands going to her hips.

Petra snatched her boots back up and began to stuff her feet back into them. "I'm not ready yet. I want to be prepared."

Maisie flung her arms down, then strode toward the door, her eyes stinging. "Fine."

"Maisie," Petra called. "I'm sorry. I just—I'm not ready yet. Maybe the note scared me a little. How about tonight? I've got those interviews for the open serving position this afternoon, so maybe after dinner?"

"All right," Maisie said, pausing with her hand on the doorknob.

"Maisie," Petra said. "I know this is a big clue, I just want to be prepared for it. I'm sure we'll figure out where Jiordan is now. He's not—I don't think he's dead."

"Me either," Maisie mumbled. And then she couldn't hold the tears back any longer. She pulled a lace handkerchief from her pocket and dabbed her eyes before turning around.

Petra came over and grabbed her hands. "We will find him. I promise."

Maisie forced a smile. "Well, Jiordan wouldn't thank us for ruining the reputation of Everturn's Finest Tea Shoppe; we'd better get back down there and get the place ready for opening tomorrow. One day closed is long enough."

Maisie was ready to leave the room and get away from the trunk. Her mind had just jumped to the worst idea. She wanted to stop thinking about how it was plenty big enough to hold a body.

Three

PETRA

The Boxton Inn was down on the Low Rise, close to the harbor. The house-sized lifts from the First Rise down to Low were busy as always, as people flocked to and from the docks. The smell of mechanical grease and steam overpowered the scent of the horses teamed to the carriage Petra had to cram herself next to in the enormous lift. She had a perfect view of the harbor and the entire Low Rise as they descended, though; the tiny warehouses and inns growing larger as she grew closer. The ships at the docks teemed with activity she could see even from here as she clutched one of the wrought-iron bars enclosing the lift.

Petra had cancelled all of her interviews this afternoon by means of several quick notes passed along by courier. Maisie was busy in the kitchen decorating cakes again and wouldn't notice she was gone, with frosting up to her elbows. She felt bad for going without her sister, but Petra wanted to get some answers first before they tried to open the trunk. Unfortunately, that meant Evan.

Tucked inside her coat pocket was a rare Amaryllian amulet she had borrowed from her father's workshop. She obviously couldn't plant the quartz to spy on Evan, but with any luck, he wouldn't know a truth amulet if he spotted one. She had considered wearing it around her neck, but she wasn't entirely sure whether the amulet was illegal in Harrowdel or not. She certainly didn't want any thieves getting ideas. So she kept the gold spherical amulet in her pocket.

Evan met her in one of the private parlors on the ground floor of the inn. The tavern keeper brought them plain black tea and biscuits at Evan's request. He grinned at her when at last the door shut, leaving them in private in the small but cozy room. They sat in the wooden chairs beside the small table, a Scitican rug under their feet, the original colors long worn away. Petra's back was to the window that overlooked the harbor, making her only a little uncomfortable.

"I take this visit as a sign you're having second thoughts about working for me? How come you didn't bring your charming sister?"

Petra scoffed, then eyed the biscuits.

"They're not poisoned," he said with a wink.

She glared at him and ate two. "I don't need to work for you. And this is just between you and me right now. But I do need—your—help," she said reluctantly.

His eyes lit up and he grabbed his glass of tea. "Do go on."

"The trunk. It won't open."

She had tried as soon as they had brought it upstairs after Evan left the shop and Maisie had gone down to use the loo. She was sure Maisie was on the verge of giving up hope, and Petra wanted to be prepared for when they opened it together. She really needed the trunk to give them some answers—answers that pointed to Jiordan being alive. After so many dead ends, and the latest letdown with the Harrowdel Gazette, she didn't want to mess up this big lead. But to get into the trunk, she needed—

"Mr. Rosslyn," the tavern keeper interrupted as he opened the parlor door and bowed slightly. "My apologies, but there is a Miss Everturn demanding to see—"

Maisie barged into the parlor, and her mouth opened in a little "o" of surprise at the sight of Petra.

"Shall I bring another glass?"

"That would be wonderful," Evan said, grinning.

After they were alone again, Evan spoke. "To what do I owe this immense pleasure?" The emerald in his ear glittered in the afternoon sunlight blazing through the parlor windows, and Petra noticed his eyes were a curious amber color.

Maisie looked at Petra for a moment. "Well, we wanted your help."

"Yes," Petra said, tense. "We did." She tried not to feel guilty for coming here without telling Maisie; they both, after all, had done the same thing.

"Can't get the trunk open?" he inquired, a smirk visible behind his outrageous beard.

Maisie shook her head.

"I'm not surprised. Jiordan was deeply involved in the search for the Mirror. There are... certain people who would spy, steal, and kill to get their hands on it. Did he leave some sort of clue to help you open it perhaps?" he prompted.

"You probably saw it," Maisie said. "There's a strange scene carved on the lid of the trunk."

"Ah, yes. I did notice that. The lion and the peacock and whatnot?"

Petra nodded stiffly. "Any idea what it could mean?"

"I'd have to inspect it closely. In our circles, these kinds of tableaus are heavily steeped in metaphor and symbolism. Especially when alchemy is involved."

A huff escaped Petra, until she remembered she had the Amaryllian amulet. She stuck her hand in her pocket and wrapped her fingers around it. It was cold. If a lie were to be uttered in its presence, it would warm up. She knew there was some strange substance at its core, she just didn't know its scientific composition. Her father had assured her it was genuine when he brought it home from one adventure or another, but had never explained how it actually worked.

"Are you sure you don't know what happened to Jiordan?" Petra said, fingering the sphere.

"As I've said, I've been searching for him myself. We were friends."

The amulet remained cold. Petra's eyebrows rose. "Very well," she snapped. "Come by the tea shop tonight—eight o'clock—and you can look at the trunk."

She tugged her jacket straight as she stood, and Maisie followed her out of the parlor.

"Well that's something, then," her little sister said.

Petra fidgeted with her long hair as she walked. "Look, I'm sorry I—"

"There's nothing to apologize about," Maisie cut across her swiftly.

"I just wanted to be ready for when we opened it together," Petra admitted. She took a deep breath and worked to unclench her jaw.

"I know. But you can tell me these things, you know? You don't have to get everything perfect the first time. We don't always have to have a plan."

Petra snorted.

Maisie went on, "We're in this together, Petra. We'll figure it out. We'll find Jiordan."

"I know, and I'm still sorry for going to Evan without you."

"Well then let's agree not to keep anything from each other about Jiordan's disappearance. We'll figure it out together."

"All right," Petra agreed. "Evan's going to help us with the trunk, and we'll figure it out."

Maisie nodded. The smell of the harbor faded as soon as they reached the lifts. They didn't speak as they waited for an empty lift up to the First Rise.

The plateau wall at the base of the First Rise was covered in metal rails and gears, and dozens of house-sized lifts that crawled up and down. The First Rise had the most traffic, and the most lifts. As one got to the top of Harrowdel's rises, the lifts were less abundant, but also cleaner and more elegant. People said the lift to the Sixth Rise was made of gold and marble. Petra normally never went higher than the Fourth Rise. There was nothing stopping her, she just couldn't be bothered, never having any business up there.

Both deep in thought, the girls walked back to Cordial Crescent upon reaching the First Rise. Maisie's short heels clicked on the cobblestones, but Petra's boots were quiet.

They reached Cordial Crescent and the sight of the tea shop eased Petra's headache a little. Her head had been aching ever since this morning when they had received the trunk and note. But the tea shop—home—was always a beacon of happiness. The large wooden sign that hung above the door, the letters hand-carved and gilded with gold paint, the flowers in the window boxes that Maisie worked hard to keep alive, and the scent of tea and pastries that seemed to waft over the entire street once it came into view. It all reminded her of her parents, and the times they had spent together as a family, when no one was off on some far-flung adventure. It was the nicest shop on Cordial Crescent, though the tailor and produce shop on either side might disagree.

"What happened to those interviews anyway?" Maisie finally asked when they turned down the narrow alley beside the tea shop.

"They'll come tomorrow instead," Petra replied. "Since we closed today, I thought we could go another day without—"

She threw out a hand to stop Maisie. There were banging noises coming from the staircase leading up to their attic. Maisie turned to look at her, eyes wide. No one from the shop would ever trespass into their private quarters, let alone make all that noise as if dragging something immense down the stairs.

"The trunk!" Petra hissed. Her pistol was already in her hand. She and Maisie rushed to the side of the covered staircase and flung their backs against the wall. Petra could feel two sets of footsteps and the occasional bang of the trunk as it hit the walls.

"Do that again, you great buffoon and I'll cut your ears off," a woman's voice growled.

"Sorry, ma'am," a man mumbled.

Petra glanced at Maisie, who looked petrified. They had never been robbed, despite the tea shop holding such vast treasure from all over the world. The reputation of the Everturns had held any would-be thieves at bay.

Petra held her pistol to her chest, wishing, just as she was sure Maisie was, that they had more firepower.

The door at the bottom of the staircase swung open, hinges groaning.

A tall man with greying hair carried one end of the trunk as he backed out the door. Petra aimed her pistol at him. He spotted her and froze. The heavy trunk slipped from his hands and banged on the cobblestones.

"What now?" the unseen woman asked irritably. The other side of the trunk lowered.

Maisie came close behind Petra. "That's our trunk you're stealing," she said. "We've all rights to shoot thieves."

From the shadows of the staircase came a thin woman, a red hooded cloak hiding her face. "Is that right?"

The woman advanced on them, brushing past the man. The hood of her cloak furled back a little, and Petra could see a blood-red ruby right where the woman's left eye should be. Her finger on the pistol's trigger froze.

"Yes, I thought so," the woman said softly.

Petra couldn't look away from the entrancing ruby eye. Everything in her vision became red. Like blood soaking into everything around her. Then a bright flash erased everything, and she fell.

Four

MAISIE

Everything was still red. And painful. Her head throbbed something fierce. It was this that caused her to open her eyes, and she realized the red she had been seeing was the inside of her eyelids. She and Petra lay under the glowing streetlamp outside their staircase. It was night.

"Petra!" she shouted, getting to her knees and scrambling over to her sister.

Her sister woke and flung her long dark hair out of her face. The pistol still in her hand swung about wildly.

"What the—where—what happened?"

Maisie got to her feet and offered Petra a hand up. "That ruby-eyed—*witch lady* and her goon stole Jiordan's trunk!"

"That's what I thought," Petra said, clutching her head with one hand. "I just hoped I'd imagined it. Did you see that..."

"Red? And then the flash?" Maisie said, shuddering.

"I've never seen anything like it. And the ruby. Eugh, what was that about?"

"No idea. Come on, let's get inside. Do you have any idea what time it is?"

Maisie shook her head. It was dark, and with the shop closed, it was silent inside the building anyway. They bounded up the stairs. The door at the top had been left open.

"Oh no! Biscuit!"

Maisie leapt behind her folding panel and searched, rifling through piles of clothes, and peering under her bed. Their cat was nowhere to be seen. During the day they kept him locked in the attic, but let him roam the tea shop at night to hunt any mice that got in.

"I'm sure he'll come back," said Petra, who was looking around their attic in distaste.

Maisie thought she knew why. She felt violated. Their private space had been entered by strangers who had been intent on stealing from them. Not to mention the violation of knocking them unconscious and leaving them lying in the alley. And that ruby eye...

"But he's never been outside of the shop before," Maisie worried, flopping down on the carpet. "And it's been hours!"

They heard banging coming from the front of the shop. Maisie jumped. "What now?" She got to her feet and grabbed Evan's pistol off the top of her dresser. She really ought to start carrying one around like Petra always did, she thought.

"Let's go see," Petra said, and they headed downstairs to the tea shop.

All the lights were off except a warm glow coming from the doorway of the kitchen. The smells of scones and tea still lingered in the air, as they always did. A dark shadow loomed at the front door.

Petra marched to the door, Maisie on her heels.

"Who is it?" Petra demanded. "What do you want?"

"It's me, Evan."

Petra grunted and opened the lock.

"Why all the guns?" Evan asked, hesitating at the threshold, his hands raised slightly. "I thought you invited me here?"

Petra stalked away and Maisie lowered the pistol. "Come in," she said. "It's not you, it's—we were robbed."

"What?" Evan said, his brow furrowing. He entered and Maisie locked the door carefully behind him.

"The trunk was stolen," Petra deadpanned from a nearby table. Evan joined her, while Maisie went behind the tea counter to put a kettle on. She could certainly use a cup of tea right now.

"Do you know who—?"

"A lady with a ruby where her eye should be, and her grey-haired goon," Maisie said, placing the kettle on one of the five state-of-the-art burners behind the counter. Gas flickered to life at the touch of a switch.

Evan made a choking noise. "A ruby eye—oh no. No, no, no, no. She—are you sure?"

"Why? Who is she?" Petra asked sharply.

Maisie put her elbows on the counter and leaned over.

"I don't know who she is exactly," he said. "But I've heard plenty of rumors of the woman who controls the—erm—but I don't even know her name."

"Controls the what?" Petra said in a deadly whisper.

A sharp whistle sounded and Maisie jumped. She spun around and removed the kettle from the burner.

But Maisie was no longer interested in making tea.

"Who was this woman, and why would she take Jiordan's trunk?" Maisie asked.

Evan looked around, not meeting either of their eyes. Finally, he sighed and said, almost whispering, "Have either of you ever heard of the Guild of the Rose?"

They both shook their heads.

"No, well, you probably wouldn't have. It's like a secret society—no, it *is* a secret society, the oldest in Harrowdel. And not just Harrowdel; they're all over the world. Anyway, the Guild of the Rose studies alchemy, among other things. And the Mirror, the artifact your brother—and I—are looking for, it's a real-life alchemycal artifact."

Petra scoffed. "No wonder it sounded ludicrous."

"You think the woman with the ruby eye is something to laugh about?" Evan asked. Petra raised an eyebrow and didn't speak further. "She's part of the Guild of the Rose. Pretty high up in the ranks, so to speak, from what I've heard. I haven't been able to find out much, mind you—they *are* a secret society after all—but I heard they were looking for the Mirror just before I left Amaryllia."

"I bet that woman knows what happened to Jiordan," Maisie said in a rush. "Maybe—maybe Jiordan did find out something about that Mirror! But now they've got the trunk." She bit her lip. "We've got to get it back."

"No, no, hold up," Petra said, advancing on Maisie at the tea counter and towering over her, leaving Evan on the other side of the shop. "We are not going and confronting that ruby-eyed witch lady. We are not messing around with this guild, or that woman."

"What?" Maisie hissed. "That trunk was our only clue about Jiordan's whereabouts! That scene on top, I'm sure it was a clue, even if we couldn't get it open. If we don't get it back, we'll never find him!"

"I said, we're not doing it. Secret societies? Alchemysts? How are we supposed to get involved in all that? The print shop was one thing, but this? It's way too dangerous!"

Fuming, Maisie turned to grab the kettle and slammed it on the tea counter on a cast iron trivet. She grabbed tea tins and cups at random off of shelves, hardly able to think she was so mad.

Evan stepped up to the counter, fidgeting with the chain of his pocket watch. "Actually, the image on the trunk isn't, uh, totally lost to us."

The sisters both looked at him. Maisie put down the tin she was holding.

"I, uh, took a rubbing off the image before I delivered the trunk to you this morning," he said reluctantly.

"Really?" Maisie said, leaning forward onto the counter, ignoring Petra's hostile scoff.

Evan pulled a folded sheet of thin paper from the inside of his overcoat and unfolded it carefully, away from Petra, as if he feared she might rip the delicate tracing paper from his hands. He glanced up at Maisie.

"But this is wonderful!" she said, smoothing down the edges of the paper and gazing over the image. The charcoal had captured most of the design as Maisie remembered it, but she could tell some of the finer details had been lost.

"I studied it this afternoon after you both came to see me." He tugged nervously at the emerald in his ear. "Though, I was hoping to look at the original again this evening since some of the details are vague."

"What does it all mean?" Maisie asked, entranced.

"Well, these are all alchemycal symbols," he said, pointing out each one. "The peacock can symbolize achieving the goal of transmuting something—changing one thing to another—or it can refer to the process of obtaining a unique result."

Petra said tersely, "And what do *you* think it means?"

Evan rubbed his hands together. "Well, it could mean he *achieved* his goal of finding the Mirror, thus *obtaining* something. But we have to interpret the whole tableau. See the phoenix hiding behind the tree? The placement is a bit strange, but a phoenix usually represents rebirth and purification.

"And then of course, there's the seven planets, which *has* to refer to the Mirror." He pointed at the strange symbols Maisie didn't recognize, all circled around the pool of water. "Seven planets, representing seven metals."

"Why does that mean the Mirror?" Maisie asked. "And what does the water mean?"

"The Mirror is said to be made from all seven metals—an impossible feat, of course. How could you even mix quicksilver with lead, gold, tin, and the others? The water." He shook his head. "It could make the connection to the planet Mercury, to quicksilver, or could just mean the opposite of fire. And then up here, the black raven represents... well, death," he ended awkwardly.

Maisie stared at the raven in the top left corner. It had something in its mouth, but she couldn't tell what it was. A seed or something, she thought.

She didn't want to think about death. She stared at whatever might be in the raven's beak, knowing it must be important. Hoping it would mean that the raven symbolized a different death. Not Jiordan's.

"But the lion is confusing," Evan went on. "It was *blue*. The lion normally symbolizes strength, courage, or royalty—and the color gold. And it's not like he didn't have gold paint—the whole section around the sun used it, I recall. I couldn't find anything in my books for what it might mean, though my traveling collection isn't large."

Maisie perked up. "What about Father's collection?"

Petra shot her a glare but didn't say anything.

"Why not?" Maisie said, "Let's take this downstairs to his workshop and look. I bet there's plenty of books on alchemy, though I've never really looked at them all."

To Maisie's surprise, Evan took a step back, looking almost scandalized. "Really? Mr. Everturn's workshop? I couldn't possibly trespass—" he said.

Maisie snorted and came around the tea counter, grabbing the tracing and Evan's arm as she did so. "It's fine. You have my permission to look at Father's collection. Besides, you're helping us find Jiordan. I want to look up all these symbols myself."

She led Evan through the back of the tea shop to the cellar door just off the kitchen. "Wait here," she told him, then went around the corner to retrieve the key from its hiding spot between her cookbooks on a kitchen shelf. She spotted Petra standing behind the tea counter making use of the boiled water and filling a teapot, her head bent over the rising steam.

Maisie unlocked the door and slipped the cellar key into her skirt pocket.

"Are you sure you don't mind?" Evan asked, his eyes wide, as if not daring to believe them.

"Yes, come on, it's fine." Maisie switched the small brass lever that turned on the cellar lights, illuminating her father's workshop below. They could now see parts of it through the gaps in the spiral staircase that led down. Her father had been the first to install electric lights in his shop on all of Cordial Crescent back when they first became available. She lifted her skirts and led the way down.

"I'm sure there's some alchemy books down here somewhere," Maisie muttered, wandering over to the longest wall, which was covered in sturdy oak bookshelves. She sighed and started browsing, breathing in the scent of paper and lemongrass that always reminded her of her father. It had been almost a decade since he had left them, but when she was in his workshop, it was as if he had never gone.

There was the long wall of books, carefully sorted by subject, then author; the mismatched end tables, display cases, and chairs, all handpicked from somewhere different, each with their own story; the tapestries, paintings, statues, vases, and other objects collected from around the world, more valuable than the ones that decorated the tea shop upstairs; the workbench on the far wall, with the assortment of tiny wooden drawers, each containing some ingredient or artifact; and in the center of it all, the map table. It was an immense oak table, its surface a map of the world protected by a sheet of glass. Beside the table stood a wooden case full of even more maps, rolled up and labeled in their cylindrical compartments.

Maisie laid the tracing on the map table, smoothing out the delicate paper. She tried to focus on the tiny object in the raven's beak, but even with the special electric lighting focused on the table, she still couldn't make it out. The rubbing just didn't have the detail. She needed to see the trunk again to know what it was.

After a moment, she looked up to see Evan paused on the bottom rung of the spiral staircase, mouth open as he gazed around her father's workshop, staring at the collected items. When he saw her looking, he cleared his throat and took the last step down, then began browsing the bookshelf wall.

"What about your sister?" he asked, his finger hovering off the line of books he was inspecting, as if afraid to sully them with his touch.

"She's making tea. It's kind of what we do."

Evan tugged on his pocket watch chain and went back to browsing the books. Maisie wandered over to her father's workbench, where a small selection of books stood stacked untidily in the back corner, no doubt Jiordan or Petra's doing. Maisie always put her father's books back where she found them, though it wasn't often that she went through his books at all.

She heard Evan gasp and say to himself, "The golden scroll he uncovered in Scitica! Amazing; I never thought I'd see such a thing..."

Maisie chuckled quietly and picked up the book on the top of the pile, recognizing it as the one Petra had used to build the projector for the Talmanian quartz. The next book was a journal of some kind, published by another adventurer. Then there was a collection of fairytales from Rancozzi. Maisie went back to the journal, wondering if Jiordan had been reading it sometime before he had left for this last fateful expedition, and if there might be any clues about the Mirror in it.

She looked up as she heard Petra on the stairs, carrying a tray of tea things. Evan had pulled up a wooden stool at the map table and was perusing a stack of books he had selected already. Maisie brought over the journal and joined him.

"What I'm wondering," Petra said as she set down the

tea tray, "is why Jiordan would carve such obvious clues onto the outside of the trunk in the first place? Where anyone could see them and interpret them? They can't possibly point to where that Mirror is, anyway."

Maisie made a sound of agreement, then poured tea for everyone since Petra still hadn't. "Maybe it's supposed to be a distraction? A false trail of clues?"

Petra nodded. "He could be in hiding, with or without this Mirror—"

Maisie gasped. "—Maybe someone was after him! Maybe he really did find the Mirror, and his life was in danger, so he went into hiding. *Maybe* the trunk is a clue to where Jiordan is!"

"But then why would he put it there for anyone to see?" Petra pointed at the tracing.

Maisie took a sip of tea and stared at the paper; her sudden inspiration gone just as quickly as it had arrived. Petra had made a strong pot of Amaryllian Mint green tea, not one of her usual choices, but it was new, and they had to try them all. The cool mint cleared her head a little as she studied the tracing again.

"The Mirror is definitely a factor," Evan mused. "The symbols all around the pool of water indicate that. Whether he found it, I really don't know. The last time I met with him, he had been in the dark just as much as I was." He ducked his head.

"Well, if we go looking for the Mirror," Maisie said, "Maybe that's how we find Jiordan."

Petra set her teacup down with a loud clatter.

"Absolutely not. Not if that ruby-eyed witch is after it, too. I told you, it's too dangerous."

"But that witch lady stole Jiordan's trunk, for goodness' sake! We get the trunk back and we try to figure out where the Mirror is—one way or another will lead to Jiordan."

"No," Petra said. "Maisie, this is different than spying on the printer or questioning the captains on the docks. That woman had some sort of weird—I don't know if it was *magic*, but we should not go tangling with her. We could be putting the shop—and ourselves in danger."

"Petra, we need to get the trunk back," Maisie said hotly. "We can't figure out what the tableau means from just this tracing. You can't make out all the details. And who knows what's even *inside* the trunk. That means we'll need to do some poking and prodding."

Petra rolled her eyes up to the ceiling. "But that poking and prodding could lead us back to that woman, or this guild Evan mentioned—I say we try and figure out what's here on the paper, and go from there. We're not going to try looking for that ridiculous Mirror just yet."

Evan chuckled lightly and said, "I've been looking for it for years now, we're not just going to find it like *that*." He snapped his fingers. "I'd run out of clues before Jiordan even disappeared. Everything in Amaryllia was a dead end for me, but perhaps he found something."

Biting her lip, Maisie looked down at the journal she had grabbed. She couldn't believe Petra was being so controlling over this. "Petra, the drawing will only get us so far. We'll need the trunk back."

"But not right now," Petra said through clenched teeth.

Maisie looked away from her older sister and flipped open the journal. Petra was wrong. Jiordan had sent that trunk, and now the ruby-eyed witch could be opening it up, interpreting the tableau, and finding Jiordan and the Mirror. And Maisie and Petra would be stuck down here studying maps and symbols trying to *prepare*.

While Petra and Evan flipped through the stack of alchemycal books Evan had brought over, Maisie studied the journal. There was nothing else she could do now, and perhaps one of them might find some clue that would get them started on figuring out this dangerous puzzle.

The tea in her cup had long since gone cold by the time she finished skimming through it. The alchemy books had only cemented Evan's interpretations of the trunk tableau, but offered no clue as to the blue lion, or where Jiordan or the Mirror might be. Maisie continued flipping pages in the journal until she reached the very end, and heaved a sigh when none of the writing or drawings yielded any clues she needed. She tossed it onto the map table.

Petra had retired to the chaise lounge along the wall opposite the bookshelves, a book she had pulled at random in her fingers. Evan was still hunched over the map table examining a new set of books that he had pulled, their subjects only loosely related to alchemy. Maisie closed her eyes in a long blink, then snuck a look at

Petra. Her sister was struggling to keep her eyes open, her finger trailing along the page as she stared at it. Maisie opened her mouth to suggest they give up for the night, but lowered her eyes instead.

She knew Petra was just trying to protect them. And if Petra's idea of deciphering the tableau was what tethered her to sanity, Maisie would let her go about it. Obviously, Petra wanted to find Jiordan as much as she did, but for as long as she had known her sister, Petra was always one to make her own plan her own way.

If Petra stopped planning and looking, she would fall apart. As long as Petra was focused on finding Jiordan, she would keep going. Petra thought Maisie couldn't handle what would happen if they stopped looking, but Maisie knew the real reason behind Petra's mania. It was to protect herself.

Her eyes downcast on the map table, Maisie's gaze wandered to the back of the journal she had fruitlessly searched. There was a small black insignia on the back corner she hadn't noticed before. Slowly she slid the journal closer across the glass surface. It looked like nothing more than a round blob until she brought it nearer. A five-petaled rose, surrounded by what looked like sun rays made of thorns. She squinted at it, wondering why it looked familiar.

She reached over to the tracing of Jiordan's trunk automatically, as she and the others had done many times that night. Again, she scanned the charcoal tracings, but the rose shape was not there. Where had she seen it before?

And what was it?

Spotting a swallow of tea left in her cup, she downed it, the cold minty liquid sending a jolt down her spine as she perched herself straighter on her stool. Petra and Evan had their noses buried in their books, and Petra's nose was so deep in hers that Maisie suspected she had drifted off to sleep. Maisie peeled open the journal again, swiftly flipping through, scanning for the rose symbol. About three quarters of the way through she spotted it. It was faint, drawn in the margin on a section the adventurer had written about a trip from Adonia to Amaryllia. She read the page again, finding nothing to define the symbol, until she reached the last sentence: " *Whereupon the Gilde der Rosen in Amaryllia welcomed me, however, I suspect the Adonia chapter overinflated the importance of my alchymy research to them.*"

Maisie blinked. The Gilde der Rosen. The Guild of the Rose. Of course. She flipped the journal over to look at the dark insignia again. Her gaze drifted to land on the tea tray Petra had brought down, with the scones Maisie had baked with the currants she had purchased up on the Third rise the other week. And she remembered where else she had seen the Guild symbol before.

Five

MAISIE

The clock tower square on the Third Rise was full of bright sunshine and gloomy morning faces when Maisie arrived there the next day.

Last night she had shepherded Petra up to their attic bedroom several hours after midnight. After asking Evan if he wanted to stay for the night on the chaise in her father's workshop, he seemed to wake up enough to make it down to his lodgings on the Low Rise, his flattered protests quiet but vehement.

They had decided to close the tea shop for another day for their not-quite mourning of Jiordan, but they would have to get back to work soon before they lost all of their customers. So, Maisie had planned a day of baking, and told Petra she was going out early for supplies.

She cringed at their conversation only yesterday to not keep secrets from each other about Jiordan. And it was *she* who had made Petra promise to tell her everything. And here she was, looking for the Guild symbol.

But Petra wouldn't listen to her. They were going to need to find the trunk eventually, or start looking for the Mirror to find Jiordan. And it wasn't like she was doing anything big; she was just going to look.

In the center of the square stood the clock tower, a beautiful stone structure supported by elaborate columns, so people could pass right under it. A fountain played in the northern corner of the square, the tinkling water a soothing backdrop to the shuffling morning traffic.

Maisie had passed through the square only a few weeks ago after purchasing some candied violets for a cake, when a sudden downpour had struck. She had taken refuge under the clock tower to shield the sugared violets. She never would have noticed the symbol if she hadn't been stuck under there for nearly an hour. One of the stone bricks in the center of the underpass had been carved with the rose and sun made of thorns that she now knew was the emblem of the Guild of the Rose.

She entered the throng of people going about their morning business and approached the clock tower. The enormous brass and iron timepiece clicked loudly as the minute hand moved over high above.

She adjusted the empty sack on her shoulder, her excuse for leaving the tea shop; she had told Petra she needed more rose petals for their most popular scones. Petra would be spending the day catching up on her interviews for their new server and had merely waved as Maisie left.

In her skirt pocket she had tucked the sketch of Evan's charcoal rubbing, which she had copied sometime last night. Evan had grudgingly agreed to leave the rubbing in the workshop, where Petra and Maisie had locked it in the family safe. If the ruby-eyed witch raided the tea shop again, it would at least be safe. Also in her pocket was Evan's borrowed gun. She kept meaning to return it to him, but she rather liked its slim design, which fit perfectly in her deep dress pocket. She'd ask him later if she could borrow it long-term—or at least ask where he had gotten it.

Around her neck swung a large gemstone she had taken from her father's workshop that morning. Maisie had worried all night about the ruby-eyed woman—how could they possibly defend themselves against her? She had carefully removed the black gem from where it hung between bookcases and slipped it around her neck. It was shaped like a pendulum, and she remembered her father telling her it was a Pruvian protection amulet he had gotten on his first expedition there. It had been a gift from a village shaman, who promised the gemstone possessed ancient protective energy. She knew Petra thought some of their fathers' artifacts were hokey—if she couldn't understand the science behind them—so Maisie had taken it for herself. If anything, it eased her nerves. A piece of her father's protection. She tucked it into her bodice so it wouldn't swing about as she walked across the square.

Maisie stopped under the cool shadow of the clock tower, pretending to adjust the buckle on her shoe. The rose carved into the central stone was worn from foot traffic, but it was just as she remembered. The round five-petaled rose with the rays of thorns circling it. Slowly she stood and surveyed the rest of the area under the clock tower, though she was quite familiar with it after her stint in the rain. *If anyone accosts me*, she thought nervously, one hand on the gun in her pocket, *I'll tell them I'm meeting someone here*. She didn't know anything about the Guild of the Rose, but their encounter with the ruby-eyed witch lady was enough to give her a healthy dose of fear.

Fear can be a good thing, her father had always liked to say when recounting his adventures. *Fear can keep you going when nothing else can. Fear can protect you, and motivate you—so long as you don't let it overpower you.*

Maisie threw back her shoulders and glanced around the bustling courtyard, looking for more signs. If the insignia were here under the clock tower, would it lead her to the Guild? From the note in the journal, she knew there was a chapter in Adonia, and it would only make sense that it was in Harrowdel, the capital. Was it on this rise? Her gaze roved around the courtyard, and she spotted the fountain in the north corner, the morning sun casting a cold shadow on it, the petal-like curves of the stone fountain throwing their own shadows. *Petals*, she thought, stumbling toward it, hitching up her bag.

The stone fountain was a rose. Trying to look casual, she strolled around it, looking for more insignia. Perhaps one of the petals would lead her in the right direction, but which one? There were five, each pointing down a different street leading off the square. But then she realized the stones under her feet made a circle around the fountain, and *there, yes!* What could be rays of sunlight represented in opposingly-placed bricks. How had she never noticed before?

"And this one..." Maisie muttered to herself as she walked around it, stopping at a brick that was longer than all the others. It pointed directly down a narrow lane leading off the square. Septon Street. She glanced over her shoulder before lifting her chin and heading toward the street.

A hand grabbed her arm before she reached the shadow of Septon Street. Thinking the Guild of the Rose must have been watching her, she meekly turned to look over her shoulder, hoping they would take pity on her and let her in to their headquarters anyway. But it wasn't some aging alchemyst clutching her arm. It was the ruby-eyed witch.

"And just where do you think you're going?" the woman crooned. Her hood was up, but Maisie could still see the ruby embedded in her left eye socket. Dark curls spilled from under her hood, and her full lips were as red as the gem.

"Nowhere," Maisie said, her fingers flexing on the pistol in her pocket. "Get off of me."

"Right," the ruby-eyed witch said, pressing her nails into Maisie's arm. "I shouldn't have underestimated you, it seems. You are an Everturn after all. Of course you figured out where the entrance to the Guild was," she said, almost to herself.

"Let me go," Maisie said loudly. She didn't want to pull out the pistol in broad daylight, but none of the people rushing about the square were paying them any attention, too intent on their own business.

The ruby-eyed witch clicked her tongue, shaking her head. "No, I don't think I will. I think you're going to come with me down to the Low Rise. And I think you know what will happen to you if you don't cooperate."

Maisie bit her lip. She glanced once at the ruby and then away. She huffed and pulled out the pistol—it was now or never. She didn't care if the magistrate's guards hauled her in for it or not; she wasn't going anywhere with this woman.

Keeping the pistol in the shadow of her market bag, she pointed it at the woman's stomach, her heart racing. "I said, let go of me."

The woman laughed and looked at her with false pity. "Very cute, my dear. But pointless."

Red glow began to fill the corners of Maisie's vision, and she lost focus for only a second before turning her head away and trying to shake the feeling.

But a second was all it took. The woman yanked the pistol out of her hand, and quickly stuffed it in a fold of her cloak. Maisie fought against her, reaching out for the pistol as soon as it slipped from her grip, but her flailing elbows and scrabbling fingers got her nowhere.

"See?" the woman said. "Pointless. Now let's go. Call

for help and you'll be flat on the pavement in shorter than it takes to breathe."

Maisie stared at her open-mouthed, then took a shaky breath. Never in her life had she been threatened, robbed, or anything of the sort—before these last two days, anyway. She was an Everturn; people loved their shop, their family. They were respected. And she had never been disarmed before. *Stupid alchemy*, she thought. *It's cheating.*

"Fine," Maisie hissed. "But I don't know what you want with me on the Low Rise, and it's a long walk, so maybe on the way there you can tell me where Jiordan's trunk is and why you stole it from us."

She jerked her arm in the woman's grip, using the movement to disguise what she was doing with her other arm. Her market bag slipped off her shoulder and fell to the ground beside the fountain. She didn't know if Petra would look for her up here, but it was worth a shot.

The woman snickered and steered Maisie through the square, heading toward the lifts down to the Second Rise. There was a long line at the gate, and Maisie smirked at the ruby-eyed witch, who was clearly in a hurry.

"You could start talking," Maisie said as they idled in line, confident that the woman wasn't going to do anything to her in such a crowded space.

But with a small movement that revealed her ruby eye to the gateman, and a second movement at her coin-purse, the ruby-eyed witch had gotten them up to the front of the line. The gold in the gateman's pocket clinked when he lowered the rail to the next lift as it arrived with a grinding of gears and a hiss of steam. After everyone inside stepped out, the ruby-eyed witch stepped on, pulling Maisie with her.

The gate clanged shut, and Maisie inhaled sharply through her nose. The gateman hadn't let anyone else on. They never did that. *How much gold did she give him?*

The nails digging into Maisie's arm didn't relent, and Maisie's next demand for information died in her throat as the two of them rode the empty lift down to the Second Rise. It juddered to a halt, and the ruby-eyed witch led her out.

In silence, they traversed the Second and First Rises, and after another solitary lift ride down to the Low Rise, Maisie was really starting to panic. She had no way to contact Petra—they hadn't even passed close to Cordial Crescent as they flew through the First Rise. She had no other weapons, after all, she had only intended on looking for the Guild symbol, not fending off this insane woman.

Where was the ruby-eyed witch taking her? Would Petra even bother to look for her? She was supposed to be hiring and training their newest server at the shop, and Maisie doubted Petra would even notice her missing until late this evening, when she would find the kitchen empty.

The docks came into view, the forest of ship masts visible long before they stepped onto the wooden boardwalk that led up and down the seaside. Sailors and merchants scurried about, moving crates and ledgers, calling orders and jeers to one another. The salty scent of the ocean washed over her on a strong breeze off the water.

She backpedaled, then flinched at the sharp nails digging even more painfully into her arm. She knew she would have bruises later. "Where are you taking me?" she demanded, staring at the enormous vessels.

The woman said nothing, only yanked on her arm. Maisie planted her feet. "No! You're not taking me anywhere! Leave me alone!" Surely, one of the sailors or merchants scurrying around would hear her, help her.

The ruby-eyed witch swore under her breath, then planted herself right in front of Maisie. She looked into Maisie's face, her wicked ruby eye glowing. "Be quiet. I can *make* you get on the boat, or you can do it yourself. Make your choice."

"What boat? Why?"

Ruby light threatened the corners of her vision.

"All right, all right! I'll go!" she looked at the ground until the disorienting red light cleared.

"That's what I thought."

The iron grip on her arm resumed, and Maisie kept staring at the ground as she was dragged forward. Another set of footsteps joined theirs, and Maisie glanced up to see the grey-haired goon who had helped steal the trunk. He was dressed in a fine cream-colored suit with a tricorn hat in navy with outrageous gold tassels.

"We're ready to leave for Amaryllia, Ms. Tria," he said. "The crew will raise anchor as soon as you're aboard. That other ship is here again, and I'd like to get ahead of them for once."

"Wait until I am ready," Tria the ruby-eyed witch replied, pushing Maisie ahead of her. They approached a gang plank leading to a magnificent ship. It was one of the finest ships in the harbor, freshly painted in black and gold with most of its crisp sails furled. But no matter how inviting it looked, Maisie would not step on board. She couldn't.

Never in her life had she left Harrowdel, even though her father and brother had explored the world from Scitica to Pruvia, and up and down the wild coast of Rancozzi. She had no desire to ever leave Cordial Crescent, for that matter. No matter how much she might tell Petra it was because she loved the tea shop, ever since their parents died on the expedition to Scitica, the world had transformed in her eyes from a place of wonder to a place of death. It was no wonder Jiordan was missing.

Or dead, the thought came unbidden to her mind.

And she couldn't leave Petra all alone at the tea shop, not now of all times.

She glanced around the rest of the docks. Sailors were focused on their business, merchants had their noses buried in their wares or their ledgers, and no one was watching them approach the ship, *The Aura Aqua*, which was carved in great letters on the starboard side, gilded in gold. Another ship to the right was preparing to leave too, the sailors scurrying back and forth up the gang plank with last-minute goods.

While her attention was on the other ship, Tria pushed her onto the gang plank of the *Aura Aqua*. Maisie lifted shaking hands to the ropes on either side, glancing into the churning water below. Would her chances of escape be better if she jumped right into the water? She was a fair swimmer, fair enough to stay above water until she could hoist herself up onto one of the lower docks.

But too late, Tria shoved her onto the *Aura Aqua*, and the gang plank was pulled from shore. Tria's man called orders to the sailors Maisie didn't hear. The enormous workings of the ship reverberated up through Maisie's feet as the anchor was raised. *No*, she thought. *I can't.*

The *Aura Aqua* began to move, slowly but forcefully away from the dock.

Maisie couldn't breathe. She couldn't leave Harrowdel, unarmed, alone. She didn't care where the ruby-eyed witch was taking her; she wouldn't go. She would rather jump in the ocean.

So she did. She vaulted over the side, her cherry red skirt fluttering in the stiff wind.

As her vision filled with red, she fell like a rock toward the hard ocean surface.

Six

PETRA

"She's just back here," Petra said to her newly hired server Weston. "You'll want to stay out of the kitchen when she's baking, if you don't want to come out covered in frosting, that is." *Or burns*, she added to herself.

She led the middle-aged man back toward the kitchen, their final stop on her tour of the closed shop. Weston was an amicable gentleman, and his manners were impeccable. He didn't know a lot about tea, but that could be taught. Their best server Lin was due with her first child soon, and Khalia couldn't work every day because of her schedule. They had been hurting for a new server for too long.

"Maisie?" she called, poking her head into the kitchen before entering. Once she had nearly gotten singed by a tray of almond swirls Maisie had just yanked from the great oven and was rushing around the kitchen looking for a place to put down. Petra had learned to enter the kitchen cautiously.

But it was empty. She shrugged. "She must have stepped out," she told Weston, then sniffed. There was nothing in the oven. Nothing cooling on racks. No mess on the large battered table. Not even a plate of leftover treats.

Petra backed away from the kitchen, her heart racing. "Um," she blurted, "I'll introduce you to her tomorrow. Let's mark down your hours for today and I'll see you tomorrow morning."

Weston nodded, quietly following her to the back room where they kept the employee ledger. As Petra led him back through the empty shop, she drew a shaky breath to herself, a sudden fear jolting down her spine.

The jingle of the bell over the door sounded. Petra glanced up hopefully, but it wasn't Maisie, it was Evan.

"Come in," she said tersely.

As Weston retrieved his overcoat and hat from the peg behind the tea counter, Petra approached Evan.

"Something's wrong," they both said.

Petra's eyes widened. "Maisie's not here," she said quietly. "I don't think she's been here all day. She's never done that before. We don't even have anything fresh baked for tomorrow, not that that's really important."

Evan tugged the emerald in his ear, glancing quickly at Weston and back to Petra. "I found this up on the Third Rise." He slid a bag from his shoulder, a canvas bag with handles, the Everturn's Finest Tea Shoppe logo dyed on the front in bold black letters. It was worn with use, the lettering faded.

"We don't sell those anymore," Petra whispered, reaching out to run it through her fingers. "It's Maisie's. She told me she was going up to the Third Rise this morning to get—something for baking, but—"

She turned abruptly, sensing Weston behind her. She forced a smile. "Great job today," she managed, her teeth gritting together painfully.

Weston's greying moustache twitched, and he put his hands on the lapels of his overcoat. "Is something wrong? Would you like me to stay and serve, or—?"

Petra's mechanical smile melted a little. "No, no, everything's fine. And this isn't a customer, he's a friend. I'll see you tomorrow, though," she said, dismissing him.

Weston doffed his bowler cap and headed out the door, sending the bell jingling again.

As soon as his shadow passed out of Cordial Crescent, Petra threw the bolt on the door and yanked the curtains shut. "Do you have any idea what happened?"

Evan gently folded Maisie's market bag in half and placed it on a nearby table, then fiddled with his pocket watch. "Well," he said slowly. "I'm a little concerned that she might have found the Guild of the Rose herself."

"What do you mean?" Petra demanded, grabbing Evan's arm. The feel of his arm under her fingers surprised her, and she quickly let go.

"I mean I found the bag near the Guild headquarters."

Petra pinned him with a look, and her right fingers itched for the pistol hidden in her shoulder holster. She didn't normally carry it while working in the shop, until the day Evan had showed up, anyway. "How in the seven continents do you know where their headquarters are?"

He pursed his lips. "I—well, this morning I decided to find them for myself."

Petra narrowed her eyes at him. "I thought we'd agreed we wouldn't approach the Guild yet?"

"I didn't agree to any such thing. That was between you and your sister."

Her jaw clenched and she had to wrench it back open. *How could Maisie do this to her?* "How, then? How did you know where to look? I thought you didn't know anything about them," she added.

"I didn't. But this is what I do for a living; I find things. I never cared about where or who they were before. I didn't want to mess with them. But I figured if they knew something about Jiordan's disappearance and the Mirror too, well, I thought I would look, even if you didn't want to. And I think Maisie was thinking the same thing."

"Maisie and I—She was just—" she stuttered, then slammed her hand down on the nearest table. She was shaking. She took a breath to try and steady herself. "Well where are they, then? Let's go. If they took her—"

Evan put a hand on Petra's shoulder, and she burned him with a look until he removed it.

"We can't just go running in there," he said. "First of all, I don't know if we can even get through the door, and I'm not prepared to confront the entire Guild of the Rose of Adonia just yet, especially that ruby-eyed woman. We need to find out how to get in. What to expect if we *do* get in, and figure out how we can even go about finding Maisie. I doubt we can just ask for them to return her to us. We need to do more research first."

"Research?" Petra scoffed. "Now's not the time for research."

"Yes, research," Evan drawled. "It's what us explorers do. It's not all tromping through jungles and dusting off ancient ruins."

"Oh, it's what explorers do, is it? Wow, I had no idea what your life must be like." She looked significantly around the shop at all of her father's artifacts, artwork, and treasures.

Evan began to turn red, and he took a step back. "I mean—I *know* you know what explorers do. Your father is one of the most well-known—I'm sorry—I—"

"Maybe if you got off your high horse for a second, you could think about Maisie! They took her! You explorers purposely put yourself in this kind of danger, but Maisie? She's a baker! She didn't sign up for this!"

"I think she'll be fine," Evan said. "Maybe she's braver than you think."

Petra rounded on Evan and got close enough to smell a hint of his citrus cologne. "You don't know anything about her," she hissed. "All you care about is finding this damn Mirror!"

She caught sight of something outside the shop window and threw an arm out, pushing Evan aside. She darted toward the front door.

"Truly, I'm sorry," he said, affronted. "I'll just leave,

shall I?"

"No," she muttered. "It's Biscuit!"

"What?"

"Our cat! Well, Maisie's cat really," she said, unbolting the door and striding out into the twilit Cordial Crescent. All rage washed from her as she spotted Biscuit across the street curling around a lamppost that had just flickered on.

She glanced behind her and saw Evan follow. "Help me catch him, will you?"

"Me?" he said, taken aback. "What for? It's your cat."

"It's *Maisie's* cat. And he got out the other day when that ruby-eyed witch stole Jiordan's trunk and left our door open. Come on."

She ran her hands down the sides of her burgundy coat and gently patted her pockets wondering if she had anything on her that the cat might be interested in. Her fingers brushed against the slight bulge of the Amaryllian truth amulet still in her pocket from when she visited Evan at the Boxton Inn. *I should probably return that to Father's safe*, she thought as she signaled to Evan to approach the cat from the opposite angle.

Biscuit ignored them, more interested in rubbing himself on the lamppost, curling his tail around it like a snake. Cream-colored with small light brown spots covering his torso, the cat had been a gift from their father some years ago, brought back from a trip to Scitica as a kitten. He wasn't young, but he was cheeky.

Petra and Evan both crept forward, the cat still ignoring them. She gave Evan a look, then nodded.

"Come here, you," Petra growled, lunging for him.

With surprising agility, Biscuit leapt into the street, evading both Petra and Evan's outstretched hands. The two of them collided, and a searing pain rent Petra's forehead.

Evan clutched her shoulders, his face mere inches from hers.

Reeling from the collision, it took a second for Petra to register how close he was. His short beard was golden in this light and he smelled like citrus. Her chest swelled, and she stumbled backward, clutching her head.

"Sorry—" she said, looking away.

"—I'm sorry," he blurted. "I mean, it's all right."

They made eye contact, and Evan shrugged with half a smile. Then they both glanced at Biscuit, who was making his way lazily toward the tea shop door, which was closed.

"Quick," she said, rubbing her forehead, her cheeks feeling warm all of the sudden. "Block his way if he tries to turn around; I'm going to go open the door."

She made a wide arc around the cat and edged over to the door, her eyes watering from the collision with Evan. She pulled the door open carefully, trying not to set off the bell and scare Biscuit, as Evan chased him from behind.

Biscuit trotted through the door, and Petra slammed it shut, the bell inside tinkling merrily as she and Evan leaned against the door, both chuckling.

"You need a device for him," Evan said, "like a cat-returning device."

Petra snorted. "I'm afraid we don't have any of those

in the shop."

"You know, I know someone in Harrowdel who might be able to make you one."

"Oh, really?"

"Oh, yes. He's quite good."

"I wish we had a device to return Maisie," Petra said, and all remnants of her smile faded from her face.

Evan didn't say anything for a minute, and they just stood there leaning against the door, an early autumn breeze playing down the quiet lane.

"You know," Evan said after a moment, "that inventor I mentioned..."

"I think it's a little too late to put a bell on Maisie."

"No, I know. But he might be able to make us something to find out more about the Guild—maybe a way to figure out how to get inside their headquarters or something. You'd be astounded by this guy's imagination."

Half an hour later, they found themselves up on the Fourth Rise in a district Petra recognized as one devoted to skilled artisans. Buzzing lampposts guided their way down Luminary Lane.

The window-displays took Petra's breath away. Woven cloth, blown glass, and all manner of mechanical devices ranging from moving clockwork statues of animals to elaborate electrical lamps lined the shop windows. She didn't have much use for any of these things, but she caught herself thinking about returning to study the displays again sometime. It was past dinnertime, and the lane was filled with patrons ogling the displays just like Petra, or showing off their purchases to their companions.

They approached a roundabout at the next intersection, where a large clockwork statue took up the center. It was elegant yet disorganized. Gears and arms gently spun, rose and fell, in a mechanical dance that *must* have a rhythm to it, though Petra couldn't decipher one. Metallic spheres at the top rotated above their heads seemingly at random. Petra was just about to point it out to Evan, but he was already skipping up the steps of the shop at the corner.

The brass plaque above the door was lit up by a small bulb in the mouth of a metal raven. It read: *Montgomery J. Hartford, Inventions, Gadgets & Timepieces.*

When the door opened, Petra expected the jingle of a bell overhead, but was instead greeted by the sound of a trilling songbird. She looked up and saw another metal bird, this one a sparrow. It closed its metal beak when the door shut behind them.

It was a small shop, with perhaps the usual types of gadgets Petra expected after seeing the other shops down the lane: brass lamps, clocks with half of their inner workings on the outside instead, and quite a few plants in what looked like special pots and vases. One had a sign that said it was self-watering, and Petra watched as water poured from a copper spout that looked like a leaf to dribble on the plant.

An older man appeared from behind the counter, drawn by the sound of the trilling bird—because with the opaque black glasses he wore, Petra was sure he hadn't seen them coming.

"Monty!" Evan cried, reaching over the counter and grabbing the man's hand. He was short, the hair poking out from his narrow-rimmed hat a rusty-grey color. The silver-framed black glasses perched on his long straight nose above a moustache that retained more of a reddish rust hue.

Montgomery Hartford shook Evan's hand, and grabbed his forearm with his other hand. "Evan Rosslyn, is that you? You haven't changed a bit." He gave Evan a roguish grin. "And who is your friend here?"

"This is Petra Everturn—"

"Say no more," Montgomery said. "Say no more." He reached out a hand to shake Petra's.

She furrowed her brow, annoyed for some reason. "Do you mind taking off those glasses? You can't possibly see with them on in this light."

"Oh, my dear," Montgomery said with a chuckle, lowering the dark rims, "I can't see with them off, either."

Petra stifled a gasp, seeing a white haze over the man's eyes. "I'm so sorry. I didn't mean to be rude."

He pushed his glasses back up his long nose. "Who ever does?" he replied. "So, you're Elliot Everturn's daughter. Older or younger?"

"Older. But my brother Jiordan is older than both of us."

He ran his fingers down his rust-colored moustache. "I knew your father ages ago. He brought me some of his finds over the years, so I could study them. He always had good stories," he said with a nod.

Petra found herself smiling. "Yes, he did."

"Well, what can I do for you?" Montgomery said, glancing between Evan and Petra for all the world as if he could see them.

Evan looked around at the empty shop and whispered, "We need something to get us into the Guild of the Rose."

Seven

MAISIE

The floor wouldn't stop moving. She clenched her fingers, drawing the tips across rough wood, rough enough to splinter. Groggily, she opened her eyes. The floor *was* moving. Through a tiny rectangular window in the wooden wall facing her, she saw the horizon line bobbing drunkenly up and down, sideways then diagonally. She crammed her eyes shut again and focused on not throwing up.

She was on a ship. Leaving Harrowdel, likely leaving Adonia.

She lurched up, and found a dark corner to retch in just in time. Her dress was stiff with saltwater and thankfully stayed out of the way. Feeling slightly better, she wiped her mouth with the back of her hand and turned to study her surroundings. She blinked a couple of times in the dim quarters. They were nice. Not as elegant as the outside of the *Aura Aqua*, but they were nice enough that she felt pretty bad for retching in the corner.

The thought of it made her stomach roil again, rolling with the motion of the ship. Desperately she sought a better place and made it to the basin just in time.

"You should try looking out at the horizon."

After Maisie finished blinking away the tears that came with the vomit, she wiped her mouth on a stiff linen she found beside the basin. She turned around.

But it wasn't the ruby-eyed witch lady, Tria, nor was it her henchman. It was a little boy, perhaps ten or eleven, with warm brown skin and motley chestnut curls poking out from a cotton cap atop his head.

"Never been on a ship before?" the boy questioned, hovering in her open doorway, which she hadn't thought was open a moment ago.

"Why are you spying on me?" Maisie grumbled. "Did that—woman send you in here?"

"What woman?" the boy said, his eyes drifting to the dark corner in which Maisie had woken up. "No women on this boat except you."

Maisie wet the stiff cloth with water from a pitcher and wiped her mouth again. A quick glance out the small window made her clutch her stomach. She closed her eyes.

"You really should try looking at the horizon."

She sighed, focusing on not throwing up again. Slowly she opened her eyes and took a step closer to the wall that looked out at the ocean. She looked away. "It's making it worse."

"Try getting closer. Don't look at the side of the ship."

She did. She stood there for a few minutes and watched the horizon bob up and down, focusing on the narrow slice where the sea met the sky. Without the visual anchor of the ship to make it a sickening sight, it actually did help. She closed her eyes briefly then looked back at the boy.

"What's your name?"

"Elijah," he said, jamming his hands into his pockets. "My father's the captain," he added with a sly smile.

"Really? Does the captain know there's a girl on his ship being held against her will?"

"What? Who?" he asked with great interest.

"Me!"

Elijah cocked his head, his boyish curls flopping. "What do you mean? We pulled you out of the water after you fell off the *Aura Aqua*. I told Father to rescue you. Did you not want to be rescued?"

Maisie's jaw dropped. "This—this isn't the *Aura Aqua*?"

"Nope," Elijah replied with a grin. "We're going to beat them to Amaryllia anyway, and get all the best deals on our cargo before they even get a chance to unload. Sometimes we can make it there in less than three days even, if the wind's good."

Noticing a small stool, Maisie sunk onto it and rested her elbow on the tiny slab of wood jutting out of the wall that she supposed might be a writing surface. For the first time, she realized her shoes were missing. She was glad she wasn't wearing her best stockings, since she was covered from head to foot in sticky salt.

"Well that's a relief at least. But I don't want to go to Amaryllia," she added in a small voice.

"Why not?" Elijah asked, genuine curiosity lighting up his eyes. "It's an amazing place! The Port of Cerise has all kinds of shops with imports from all around the world. Oh, and the food—you have to try some of Mrs. Cable's cinnamon cakes, she's got a bake shop right near the docks. My father always gives me a few coins to go there whenever we make port."

A small smile quirked up the corners of Maisie's mouth. Something other than nausea made her clutch her stomach again, and she was surprised to find herself hungry, unable to remember the last time she had eaten.

Elijah picked up on her predicament. "Hungry? Me too. Let's go to the galley, we can scrape up some food. And everything's still fresh since we just restocked."

Maisie stood and looked down at herself. Her dress was wrinkled and salt-stained; her skin was sticky with dried seawater, and her stockings would be fraying soon from the rough wooden floor. Normally she didn't mind if a day of baking left her covered in flour and icing, but now she felt in bad need of a bath.

Observant as ever, Elijah said, "Maybe we can find you some spare clothes and shoes, too, and bring you back some more water to bathe."

"That would be wonderful," she replied, "I'm Maisie, by the way." She followed him out the door and into an incredibly narrow hallway. Then she gasped quietly to herself as she clutched her bodice—but the Pruvian protection amulet was still there, and her drawing of Jiordan's tableau was still in her pocket, though damp and wrinkled.

"We've never rescued a girl who fell overboard before," Elijah went on as he confidently strode down the cramped hallways of the ship. "We don't get many girls at all. 'Cept sometimes when somebody rich books passage—we're a merchant ship, not a passenger ship, but we take on passengers on occasion when the price is right. If they want their trip to be a secret, like, or if all the passenger ships are booked up and they're desperate to get somewhere."

Elijah led them up four short steps into what Maisie assumed was the galley. He started poking through cabinets while Maisie leaned against a narrow counter, thinking. *I don't have any money for passage. They won't throw me off, will they? What if I promise to pay when I get back to Harrowdel?*

"Git out of those cabinets, lad, before I stuff you into one." A harried old man hobbled into the galley from the opposite end, leaning heavily on the railing of another short staircase. He showed some surprise at the sight of Maisie, but didn't say anything as he yanked Elijah out of a cabinet and slammed it shut. "These stores gotta last the whole trip for everybody, you know that."

Elijah didn't seem bothered by this rough treatment. He shrugged. "I know, but our new passenger was hungry. Fell overboard an' all."

The old man twisted his lips, inspecting her. She

crossed her arms over her chest, refusing to feel embarrassed about her bedraggled appearance. "New passenger, eh? I didn't set no extra stores for another passenger," the old man said to Elijah, ignoring Maisie.

Elijah kicked one of the cabinets. "Garris! My father let her on board. We have stores enough."

"That's Mr. Garris to you, you little runt."

Elijah darted forward, and Garris reached out to hold him off, clearly not wanting to harm the captain's son, but not about to let him land a blow, either. Elijah kicked at him and landed one on Garris' shin.

"You little—"

Heavy footfalls on the stairs behind Maisie intruded on the fight, and Elijah retreated as docile as ever. Garris straightened and nodded respectfully at the person behind Maisie. She turned awkwardly in the cramped quarters to see an enormous black man dressed in a neatly pressed coat and trousers of dark brown, though his sleeves had been rolled up, wrinkling them. Shiny brass buttons lined the coat, and identical ones glinted from his shoes. His face was worn and weathered, but an energy shone in his eyes, and he looked like a man who smiled often—though right now he was frowning at his son.

Automatically Maisie smiled at him, and he nodded curtly at her before addressing Elijah. "Son, I want you on the deck assisting Mr. Morgan. Garris, now would be a good time to hit the books and add our new passenger to the meal schedule."

Both nodded at the newcomer and retreated out the

opposite side of the galley following their orders without comment. Maisie took a step further into the now empty galley. The man followed, squeezing himself out of the cramped hallway and into the somewhat more spacious galley.

"Captain August Ardmore, at your service madam." He gave her a slight bow.

Maisie smiled when he straightened, and her words rushed out, "Captain! I'd like to thank you for rescuing me from the water. It's so good to meet you. My name's Maisie Everturn, and I was being taken against my will onto that ship. I never intended to leave Harrowdel." *And I don't want to go to Amaryllia.*

The captain seemed to pick up on her unsaid words, as observant as his son. "We're well underway, Ms. Everturn. There's no turning back now."

His words sounded ominous, but his baritone voice soothed their impact a little. Maisie leaned back on one of the counters. "Well, I suppose there's nothing I can do about that then," she said with a sigh. "At least I got away from that woman. She was trying to kidnap me."

Captain Ardmore seemed to think this over for a minute. "I've never seen a woman aboard the *Aura Aqua* before, and certainly not one the likes of which I saw through my telescope after we rescued you. I've been in competition with the *Aura Aqua* for years; they run the same shipping lines as we do, even when we change them. I've always thought they were up to something suspicious. But their captain is a weak-chinned old man who can't keep up with us." He allowed himself a grin. "We'll get to Amaryllia before them, and you can slip your pursuer long enough to alert the port police. Shouldn't be but three days journey—two if we're lucky. And then it's back to Harrowdel once more before we move on to the coast of Rancozzi."

Maisie gave him a weak smile. She wasn't sure if alerting the police would make a difference. If the ruby-eyed witch was a big name in the Guild of the Rose, surely she had political pull in Amaryllia, too, where there was another chapter of the Guild.

"Forgive me, Miss Everturn, I need to get back to the deck. Elijah needs a stern word after disrespecting Mr. Garris like that. I'll have the quartermaster find you some essentials and clothes—though you'll have to do with sailor's rig until your dress can be cleaned. And dinner will be served at the sound of the bell in a few hours, but—" he opened a cupboard near the ceiling, an easy feat for him— "this should hold you over until then." He handed her a rough biscuit from a burlap sack. Behind the biscuits, Maisie saw all kinds of sacks neatly labeled *flour, sugar, salt*.

"Captain Ardmore," Maisie said, accepting the shapeless biscuit and glancing at the floor. "I'm afraid I don't have any money to pay for passage. I wasn't planning on taking a sea voyage today."

The captain cleared his throat.

"But I can work," Maisie went on, brightening. "I can bake. I work in a tea shop back in Harrowdel. Everturn's

Finest Tea Shoppe. Have you heard of it?"

"Oh, aye, of course—"

"Well I can bake to earn my keep," she blurted. "Would that work for you and Mr. Garris?"

He scratched his chin and thought for a moment. "It'll work for me, and Mr. Garris will work with what I tell him. It's a deal then." Captain Ardmore reached an enormous calloused hand out, and Maisie shook it. "Why don't you familiarize yourself with the galley? Our cook'll be in shortly to start dinner, so clear out before he gets in. And I'll have Mr. Garris work out a schedule so you and the cook don't have to work at the same time—not much room in here for one person, let alone two."

"That sounds great," Maisie said earnestly.

"Well, Miss Everturn, welcome to the *Scarborough*."

Eight

PETRA

"Unpack that box of little cakes right onto one of the gold serving trays," Petra told Weston. "And be careful not to smudge the icing—these pastries are costing us three times as much as usual."

Weston assured her he would take great care and retreated to the kitchen with the pastry box tied up with red and white twine.

"You'd think the bakery could give us a discount," she muttered to herself, turning back to appraise the tea counter. There were half a dozen patrons in the shop, usual for a weekday after lunch. Petra's gaze roved over the tables, noting that Mrs. Handel would need a fresh pot of tea soon.

It had been three days since she re-opened. Three of the loneliest days of her life; she had never been away from Maisie for so long. She missed her sister's dervish-like whirling around the shop with trays of pastries, her sunny outlook despite the cloudy ways of the world, and Petra even missed the mess she would make on her side of their shared bedroom. She had tidied it only a little since Maisie was gone.

But she had had to open the shop back up. Though it had felt all wrong without Maisie, she hadn't wanted to lose any more respect from their customers. She hadn't told anyone that they feared Jiordan was dead, or that Maisie was missing, so she didn't have a good public reason to remain closed.

Some of the nearby merchants thought Petra was too young at twenty to run the shop with just Maisie, and she didn't want to give anyone the impression she was all alone without any help. She had been balancing the books for years now, and pouring tea since she was little; what did it matter how old she was?

It had been a strange and lonely three days in the shop by herself, though Evan had visited each day to let her know he hadn't heard from Monty, and to drink some tea in the corner of the shop while he read some book or another.

She went behind the tea counter and put a full kettle over the correct burner for Mrs. Handel's preferred tea, white peach blossom. Her father had put in the five burners himself, and Jiordan had since rigged them so that each burner would heat different teas to different temperatures. Engraved on each was a design to signify which type of tea.

The bell over the door jingled, and Petra looked up to

see Evan ducking into the shop, his emerald stud winking in the afternoon sunlight coming in through the bright windows.

"It's ready," he said as he reached the tea counter.

Petra's mouth popped open in surprise. "Finally," she breathed. The cheerful scent of peaches wafted over her as she opened up the tea tin.

"I just got a message delivered to the Boxton Inn for me; Monty says we can pick it up at any time. You want to go now?"

"I can't," Petra said. "It's just me and the new server Weston until closing. I can't leave him alone yet."

"I can wait," Evan said, shrugging. He reached out to grab a scone off the three-tiered tray sitting on the tea counter, and Petra slapped his hand away.

"You can pay for that, if you like. I'm having to buy all of our pastries from Madam Angelford's over in Comfit Square. You wouldn't believe the expense. But you can have a cup of tea on the house, if you want," she added, feeling bad for slapping his hand away. She slid him the leather-bound book with all of their teas printed in neat lettering.

He browsed through it for a moment as he usually did, but then flipped it shut and said, "What do you recommend?"

Petra frowned, looking him over, thinking. "You might like the Scitican Chai, it's got a real kick to it."

"Spicy? No, no. I may be an explorer, but my tastes aren't too wild."

"All right. How about the Hazelnut Midnight? Do you like black tea? That one's my favorite."

"Sure."

Monty's shop was closed when they arrived.

"Are you sure he said to come by any time?" Petra asked Evan. "His hours aren't even posted in the window." She peered around to look at the window display.

Evan cleared his throat and pointed to the golden tassel hanging near the shop sign. There was another, smaller sign, lettered in tiny, neat handwriting that read: *Pull bell for* serious *after-hours inquiries only.* Evan pulled it. At first, they heard nothing, then, from beside the shop they heard a loud banging. Petra leaned off the doorstep to peer around the corner and saw a back door swing open. Monty's head popped out, black goggles glinting in the evening streetlight. "Who's there?" he called.

Evan leaned behind Petra and placed a hand on her arm to see around her. "Ah, Monty!"

"Oh, it's you. Come on back here."

Petra and Evan exchanged looks and went around the corner of the shop, following Monty through the back door and up a handful of steps. They emerged into a dimly lit workshop, full of mechanical and clockwork masterpieces, ranging from fully operational to completely disassembled, bits and gears laying on tables laid out with perfect precision. Potted plants hung from hooks all over the ceiling, though none in such fantastic pots as the ones in the shop out front. Two gas lamps spilled the only light onto the workshop, which was even larger than the storefront.

Petra spotted Monty already on the other side of the workshop, digging through a toolbox. She stepped further in, gathering her knee-length jacket closer to her, careful not to knock anything over.

"I've got it right here," Monty said, shoving a stack of books aside and clearing space on a large work table. He turned away then came back with both his hands cupped together, holding something. Petra and Evan edged closer to the table. On it, Monty laid a metallic beetle the size of a large button.

"Eugh," Petra exclaimed, taking a step back when the thing started moving. Its tiny little legs roved over the surface of the table, while its metal antennae prodded and poked. "What is it?" she asked. "Besides the obvious."

Evan had stepped closer and was examining the thing, and just as he reached a finger out to it, the beetle stopped and turned, furling open its copper wings in a clear warning.

"It's the world's best spy," Monty said simply. Petra furrowed her brow, peering at the thing from a safe distance. Monty continued, "Always overlooked, the beetle can get in anywhere. It can squeeze in through the tiniest gap. The obvious danger is that it could be stomped on if seen, but with reinforced hinges at every joint, this particular beetle will bounce right back even after being flattened—with a pre-programmed wait time so as to avoid being flattened repeatedly."

"Huh," Evan said appreciatively.

"It is fascinating," Petra admitted. "So, it can sneak into the headquarters without being noticed, but what does that accomplish? What does it do?"

Monty pushed his black spectacles further up his nose. "Ah yes. The best part. I'm always forgetting the best part. The *best part*, is that I've taken a Talmanian quartz and adapted it to be used as the beetle-bug's eyes. Are you both familiar with the object?"

Petra glanced at Evan and a smile grew at her lips. "Yes," she said, her cheeks growing red for some reason as she thought back to their first encounter.

Monty went on, "Well, the beetle-bug will record images with the adapted quartz lens, but I've also used a quality microscopic sound recorder, so you'll be able to see and hear what goes on wherever you place it to roam."

"Wow," Petra said. "How will we see what it records?"

"Ah yes," Monty said, reaching into the half-apron tied at his waist and pulling out what looked like a matchbox with one of the short sides missing. "This box is where the beetle-bug gets its charge from. Place it in there overnight before you let it loose. Then leave the box nearby when you plant it. As it loses its charge, it will seek out the box."

He opened the matchbox and Petra could see the inside was copper, not paper like the outside. On the lid it looked like there was a thin sheen of shiny black glass.

"When you retrieve the box, you can view the recordings here," he pointed to the black glass. "The recharged beetle-bug will begin transmitting them to the viewer as soon as you open the box; its antennae create the electrical spark of connec—"

A door opened revealing a pretty woman standing in a stairwell leading up. Monty stopped speaking and ran a hand down the sides of his rust-colored mustache.

The woman had a kerchief tied over her hair and dirt under her fingernails, and she carried a small ceramic pot of ivy. She smiled politely at Petra and Evan, then stepped into the workshop and gave Monty a kiss on the cheek.

"Monty dear, it's almost pitch black in here," she said, striding over to the nearest lamp. "You can't have visitors in the workshop and leave the light like this, honestly." She shook her head and placed the ivy on top of a nearby shelf, standing on tiptoe.

"Adora," Monty said tiredly. "It's *my* workshop, and they're my visitors. If they wanted more light they would have said so."

Adora turned the lamp up and half the workshop came into better view. Petra looked down to where the beetle-bug had been a moment ago, but it was gone, and so was the matchbox. She thought she saw the outline of the box in Monty's apron pocket.

The reality of what they were doing began to sink in. She was trying to spy on a powerful—and secret— organization, all so she could infiltrate them to look for

Maisie and clues about Jiordan. It was beyond illegal, it was reckless. It was dangerous. But it was necessary.

She hadn't planned it this way at all, and she'd never be here if Maisie hadn't gone missing. And Jiordan wouldn't have sent them that trunk if he weren't in real trouble. She refused to believe he was really dead. Sending that message with the trunk was exactly something Jiordan would do if he *weren't* dead, just to get their attention. And Maisie needed her help. Petra didn't have a choice anymore.

The Guild was their only lead, and she didn't care how illegal or stupid it was to try and infiltrate them. It needed to be done. She just had to do it right.

Adora flitted about the workshop lighting two more lamps and checking on some of the plants, all the while Monty grumbled about wasting lamp gas. Petra wondered why they didn't have electric lights back here like in the shop out front, but she knew some people still preferred the flickering glow of gas instead of the buzzing brightness of electric.

"Well, what is it this time?" Adora asked, returning to where they gathered around the work table. "Singing bird statue won't sing?"

Monty reached out and put a hand around Adora's waist. "Something like that," he said, and gave her a squeeze.

"I'll leave you to it, I suppose," she said, patting his hand before retreating back to the stairs behind the door. Petra thought the woman knew she was being gotten rid of. "Have a good evening, then," Adora said to Petra and

Evan, then shut the door quietly.

They waited until her footsteps on the stairs faded, and then Monty pulled the box out and handed it over the table. Evan took it.

Monty cleared his throat.

"Oh, right," Evan said, putting down the matchbox and reaching into his vest pocket.

"No, let me," Petra said, opening her coat and pulling out her billfold.

Evan grinned at her and lowered her arm. "It's on me. I'll hold onto the bug after we're done. He could come in handy. Unless you want to continue your career as a spy?" he added in an undertone.

Petra snorted and returned her money to her pocket. "Fine."

Evan handed over the money—after Petra saw him count it out, she was glad he had talked her out of it—and he took the box containing the beetle-bug.

"It'll need a full night's charge, like I said," Monty told them. "It's got barely enough charge to skitter across this table right now. Don't plant it until tomorrow, all right?"

Petra nodded, then realized she should speak and said, "All right."

"Now," Monty went on, "I've got something else for you. On the house. Just let me find it."

Evan carefully tucked the matchbox into his vest pocket and exchanged a glance with Petra. He shrugged. Petra bit her lip as she watched Monty putter around the workroom, poking about in drawers and on shelves, muttering to himself. "I know it's here. You two can have it, I never wanted it anyway."

She watched him scour the room using only his hands, clearly having long ago memorized the layout of his workshop, with a perfect memory of where he had placed every tool, gadget, gear, and wire.

"Adora must have moved it," Monty muttered from across the room, both hands in the drawer of a desk. The desk was free of clutter, not like the rest of the workshop, with papers neatly stacked in cubbyholes atop it. "Aha! I can't believe she put it here."

He returned holding up a single golden key, with an odd symbol etched on top: a five-petaled rose with thorns surrounding it like rays of the sun.

Nine

MAISIE

Outfitted in her borrowed sailor's garb, Maisie was yet again spread out on the floor of her cabin—the only place where there was enough room to lay down and study the map. Her bunk was just a cubby tucked in the wall, and she was lucky she was short enough to fit in it somewhat comfortably. The "desk" beside the chair was only big enough for a glass of water to perch on, which she had stopped doing after the second glass spilled when the ship made an unexpected lurch.

So the floor it was. Her sailor's clothes made it easy to sprawl out on her stomach, the drawing of Jiordan's trunk spread out in front of her. The only trouble was, it had gotten nearly washed out when she had jumped into the ocean.

She had borrowed a wax pencil from Elijah and tried to retrace some of the images she remembered. She had, after all, spent an entire night in their father's workshop studying the thing. She thought she had recreated all of it. But it still made no sense.

She only hoped Petra and Evan were making more headway with the map, and wondered for the hundredth time what they were doing now. She wished she had said a better goodbye to her sister yesterday morning—was it really only yesterday she had come aboard the *Scarborough*?

Maisie shut her eyes tight as an uncomfortable feeling rose in her chest, and a tear slipped out before she could stop it. *Petra must be so worried. They'll never know I'm headed to Amaryllia. How long will I even be gone? How will I get back?*

There had been no time to approach Captain Ardmore to ask about the return trip, mostly because the man was so busy. She had already spent some time baking semi-tasteless biscuits—the quartermaster refused to ration her any ingredients with which she could make anything special—or holed up in her cabin.

As she settled her gaze back on the drawing, a knock came at her door. She grinned when Elijah popped his head in, and she sat up, drawing the paper across her folded legs.

"Doing some more drawing?" Elijah asked, slumping down against the wall until he was sitting on the floor.

"Not quite," Maisie replied, pursing her lips then deciding to share it with Elijah. What was the harm? *It's not like he would know about the Guild or the Mirror.* "It's kind of a puzzle I'm trying to figure out."

She slid it across the floor between them.

He leaned in closer, propping his head in his hands, elbows on his knees. "Huh, kind of like one of those kid's books, with all the animals," he said, pointing to the peacock, phoenix, lion, and raven. "When my mother was still alive, Father would bring home books from whatever port he'd been to."

The corners of Maisie's mouth twitched up in a smile. "My father would do the same on his expeditions," she said. "One time he even brought me a kitten." She spared a worried thought for Biscuit, but there was certainly nothing she could do for the cat now, if he hadn't found his way back into the shop.

Elijah's eyes lit up. "I'd love a kitten. I'm not supposed to be nice to the ship's cats; Father says they're sailors, too, with jobs to do. Scraps and cuddles distract them from hunting rats I guess." He looked back at the drawing then cocked his head to the side.

"What is it?"

"That raven in the corner. Kind of looks familiar." He picked up the drawing and brought it closer to his face. "Is there something in its mouth?"

"That's what I thought," Maisie said in a rush, coming over to sit next to him and pointing to the bird. "A seed, maybe?"

"I think it's a rock."

"Why do you say that?"

"'Cause that's what the one stamped on some of the cargo looks like."

"Are you sure I'm allowed to be down here?" Maisie asked, lifting the handheld torch lamp a little higher to peer around the big wooden crates in the back of the hold.

"Oh yeah, it's fine. I play down here all the time. Last trip one of the passengers' sons Martho and me would climb all over the crates trying to get the highest."

Maisie was glad she had on her sailor's garb as she gingerly stepped through the damp and dusty hold. "So where did you see this raven?"

"Back here," Elijah called, running on ahead out of the lamp light. "It's way in the back. I've seen it before, too. On other trips."

She followed the sound of his voice until she spotted him sitting atop a stack of crates, legs swinging. There wasn't anything special about them, stacked beside other crates of similar size. But as she drew nearer with her borrowed torch lamp, she could see the raven stamped on the top right corner of each crate. She peered closer at one.

"It does look the same," she muttered excitedly, pulling out the folded drawing and comparing the two. "And much clearer. That's a gemstone in its mouth, I'm sure of it. I wonder what it means?"

She stared at the drawing and the raven on the crates for several minutes in silence. Finally, she puffed out a breath. "I still don't know what any of this means. The phoenix hiding behind the tree. The peacock. The ridiculous blue lion."

"Blue lion?" Elijah asked, stilling his swinging legs at last.

"Well, yeah, the original was in color. And the lion was blue for some reason."

"Huh."

"What?"

"I dunno, it just sounded familiar. Oh, I know! You remember how I said my father used to bring me all those books whenever he could get them in port?"

"Yes?" Maisie asked, excitement rising.

"The blue lion... No, that doesn't sound right. *The Sapphire Lion.* That was it! It was about this lion who was a king, of all the other animals, you know? And he was really rich; he had a whole room full of treasure, but his favorite was a rough sapphire he had found himself. And the other animals wanted his treasure—"

"Wait a minute, that sounds familiar," Maisie interrupted. "I think I read that one, too. There was a... peacock! The peacock who tried to trick him into becoming friends just to steal it."

"Oh yeah," Elijah said. "And the lion locked up his treasure and went into hiding for some reason—"

"Wasn't it he left the kingdom to get away from all the greedy animals?"

"Yeah, and he gave his friend the raven his sapphire to keep safe, because he was his only real friend or something."

Maisie's heart beat faster as she locked eyes on the raven on the nearest crate. "Holy *sugar!* Jiordan gave it to someone to keep safe before going into hiding, or on the run or something! We must still have that book at home somewhere. Oh, I wish I could tell Petra."

"Who's Jiordan?" Elijah asked.

"Oh. My brother. He's... he's been missing for months. This was a clue he gave us before disappearing. But where is *he?* Do you remember what happened to the lion in the story? I can't remember."

Elijah shook his head. "Me either. I thought he just disappeared or something to teach all the other animals a lesson about being greedy. Those stories are always trying to teach you something."

Maisie slumped down onto a crate, her thoughts spinning. Jiordan hid the Mirror with a friend, like the raven in the story. And disappeared—probably to teach the greedy alchemysts a lesson. Her gaze settled on the raven stamped on the nearest crate. "Where are these crates bound?"

"Oh, I dunno, somewhere in Amaryllia," Elijah said before hopping back down. "I could maybe check the roster sometime when my father's not in his quarters."

Maisie furrowed her eyebrows. "Are you sure? I don't want to get you in trouble with your father."

He shrugged. "I'm allowed to look in his rosters. Just never had a reason to. It's not like they're secret."

But the raven-stamped crates were nowhere to be found on the captain's rosters. Elijah came and saw her in the galley the next day while she was sliding a tray of biscuits into the oven.

"But there must be a dozen of them!" Maisie said. "How could they have missed putting them on the roster?"

Elijah frowned. "I don't think they were missed. You know how particular Mr. Garris is about inventory."

Maisie narrowed her eyes. She certainly did. Every time she worked in the galley, he poked his head in to count how many biscuits she was making, or weigh the sacks of flour. She reached onto the counter to set the timer for the oven, thinking.

She had to find out where those crates were going. And she really wanted to find out what was in them. Trouble was, she couldn't involve Elijah, even though he had helped her so much already.

Even though he said sneaking about and looking in his father's rosters was all right, she wasn't sure his father would approve of any further digging. And the last person on this boat she wanted to cross was the captain.

She would just have to do it on her own.

Ten

PETRA

Huddled over a cup of Rose Oolong tea—it was the only kind Maisie kept in the kitchen, in a frilly pink and white tin beside her cookbooks—Petra waited while Evan brought out the beetle-bug he had retrieved from outside the Guild entrance on the Third Rise.

The shop was closed, the store-bought pastries packed away as best as they could be, and Petra keenly felt Maisie's absence as the steam from the rosy tea wafted over her bowed head. She inhaled the familiar scent and closed her eyes for a moment.

"Ready," Evan said, and Petra's eyes fluttered open. He placed the fake matchbox in front of Petra and brought another chair rather close to sit beside her. He reached over to the pot of tea she had made and poured himself a cup, the steam swirling up between them.

Petra watched him sniff the tea out of the corner of her eye, and he made a pleased sort of sound before sipping it.

She reached over to open the matchbox just as Evan did the same, their fingers brushing for a brief moment.

"Oh, you go ahead," Evan said, ducking his head and pulling his hand back to clutch his teacup instead.

Petra rubbed her fingers together and then lifted the top of the matchbox.

Losing connection with the beetle-bug's antennae, the screen at the top of the box came to life, showing them what the bug recorded starting that very morning.

The view was like nothing Petra could have imagined. The scene was shown from the depths of the street gutter as the bug slipped under the door to the Guild entrance. *So, this is what a bug sees*, Petra thought, *only this one is unkillable*. She glanced fondly at the metal bug in question, then turned her attention back to watch the view as the thing scurried around a small entryway that led to a library.

She watched for the first half hour on the edge of her seat, forgetting Evan was even there. Her tea grew cold, and she was reminded of the night she and Maisie had spent holed up in the kitchen doing nearly the same thing, with such disappointing results.

But even after a few hours, the bug didn't show them Jiordan, or Maisie even, and Petra soon began to lose interest. She stared down at her cup, watching the dregs swirl in the bottom, hoping her siblings were all right. Hoping she could find some answers soon. She glanced at Evan, who was reclining in his chair with one foot propped on a knee, still watching the screen intently.

The bug didn't stumble onto anything exciting until well past midnight. Petra had no idea what time of day the bug was showing them anymore, but she had drained the last of her cold tea, and was leaning back in her chair like Evan, when she heard her brother's name.

From behind a bookshelf, the bug continued to scurry around the room it had wandered into, but they could still hear what it was picking up.

"...thought that Everturn fellow had been arrested?"

"Arrested?" another voice replied. "Well, detained. I'm tempted to go up to the Sixth Rise to headquarters just to see the famous Jiordan Everturn behind bars, myself. But we'll get to..."

And they didn't hear anything further, as the bug continued to scurry away from the conversation.

Petra sat up and slammed her fist on the table, rattling the tea things. She looked at Evan, eyes wide.

"They have Jiordan! They *have* him. He's alive!"

"It *had* to be up on the Sixth Rise," Petra muttered the next afternoon.

She and Evan were waiting in the line for the pristine lifts leading up to the Sixth Rise, which were few and far between, making the highest rise of Harrowdel seem more exclusive than it already appeared.

"Are you really surprised?" Evan replied, tipping his

hat down against the blinding light of the setting sun. His amber eyes glinted in the orange afternoon light. "The Third Rise did seem rather questionable for such a prestigious society."

Petra sighed, glancing over Evan's shoulder at the line behind them. She was anxious to get up to the Sixth.

"I hope Weston can manage the tea shop all right alone for the rest of the day," Petra said. "Lin's out for the next few months and Khalia is traveling with her mother; we've no one else."

There had been no mention of Maisie in the beetle-bug's recordings. But they knew Jiordan was there, and that was a start. She would find a way to track down Maisie, too.

"I'm sure the shop'll be fine," Evan said distractedly as the line moved forward.

If Petra had counted correctly, they should be admitted to this next open lift. Not only were there so few lifts, but the highly polished silver framework with actual marble plating made them so heavy they could only carry five passengers at a time. *What a waste*, Petra thought.

They approached a rather short woman who held the end of a velvet rope blocking their way, and they halted.

"Papers?" the woman asked, holding out her hand.

"What do you mean, papers? You didn't ask anyone else for them," Petra said through gritted teeth, roughly shoving her hand into a coat pocket for her identification.

The short older woman behind the velvet rope simpered, "Standard random checks, you know." And she took Evan's papers to examine.

Petra swaggered closer to the woman, utilizing her full height as she handed over her papers. The woman, with a small pink bow in her greying brown hair, didn't seem cowed in the least.

"Hmm," the woman said, reaching into her vest pocket to pull out a pair of spectacles.

Petra tapped her foot.

The lift operator closed the door to the waiting lift while the woman studied Petra and Evan's identification. Too soon after the lift rose without them, the woman handed their papers back.

"Looks like you'll have to wait for the next one," the woman said, falsely apologetic.

Evan stepped in between the two women as Petra's temper boiled. She brushed him aside and crossed her arms. She stared straight ahead at the wall of the plateau, which—unsurprisingly—looked cleaner than those of the lower rises. There were no loose stones at the bottom, and even the random weeds and grasses that would normally grow out of crevices had been removed.

She huffed. She had no problem living on the First Rise. But the arrogance that came with living on the higher rises—as evidenced by this woman who controlled the lifts—seemed contagious and inevitable. She had always preferred the lower rises. The people were more genuine.

Finally, they were allowed through the velvet rope and onto the next lift with three others. Petra slunk into the corner and poked about inside her coat to be sure her pistols were strapped properly. A tinkling of music filtered out from somewhere in the silver framing, no doubt some mechanical device like those in Monty's shop.

She ran her hand over the pocket that contained the golden key Monty had given them. What she hoped was the key to the main headquarters of the Guild of the Rose.

This morning, Evan had come by the tea shop early and asked to browse through her father's workshop for information on the Guild. He had brought up a couple of books and spent the whole day looking for clues about the Guild. She made him a whole pot of Hazelnut Midnight while he scoured the books, looking for anything that might come up with the bug they would need to know. And finally he had found mention of the Guild with the rose symbol on the same page in some kind of journal.

As she pulled her hand away from the key in her pocket, she realized it was shaking. Quickly she hid her hands behind her back. Were they at the top yet? She didn't like charging in like this, not knowing what to expect.

"It's going to be fine," Evan leaned over and whispered in her ear.

She whipped her head to look at him and whispered back, "I know."

"They can't possibly hold him there, legally."

"I know."

"At least he's alive."

Her throat closed up, and she nodded. For a brief

second she closed her eyes, and then felt a squeeze on her arm. She opened her eyes to meet Evan's gaze, and a breath of his citrus scent wafted over her. She looked away to see the top of the Sixth Rise cresting before them.

They came to a gentle halt—nothing like the juddering, shuddering lifts down on the low rises—and the operator at the top opened the gilded gates for them.

Petra strode away from the plateau's gold-tipped wrought-iron fenced edge, a bad taste in her mouth from the whole lift experience. Why had that lift operator at the bottom stopped them? She had never had to show identification for a lift before.

"Do you know where you're going?" Evan asked.

"Sure," Petra said, leading the way toward the nearest street. "The garden quarter is just past the museums. I've only ever been up here twice, but both times were for the museums when we were younger, and then Father would take us to see some gardens."

"Ah. I've never had the time to get up this high. I haven't spent much time in Harrowdel since I was a boy, only when fate or fortune leads me here."

"You're from Harrowdel originally then?"

"Yes, but I've made my home in Amaryllia these past few years."

"Oh. And which country did you pick up the beard in?"

Evan laughed, throwing his head back, then reached up to stroke the side of his face. "You don't like it?"

Petra shrugged, eyeing the unusual albeit well-manicured facial hair. "It's just different. Kind of takes some getting used to."

"I've never been able to fathom what Harrowdellians have against beards. In Amaryllia they're all the rage."

She smirked. "I'll take your word for it."

"Really? Well, I should also tell you that in Amaryllia, I'm considered quite handsome."

Now Petra burst out in laughter. "All right, handsome, enough messing around. We need to find the Torrence Gardens. That's where they said the Guild entrance was near."

Petra had stayed up most of the night watching the rest of the beetle-bug's recording, until she knocked over her empty tea cup when she nodded off. She had been lucky to catch someone mentioning the gardens after she jerked out of her daze.

The museum quarter was closing down as the sun dipped toward the horizon, a sight that took Petra's breath away, never having seen it from this high a rise before. The golden yellow sun was an explosion of light and color sinking into the sea at their backs. Petra stole a few glances at it as she led Evan past the immense stone facades of the various museums. There wasn't time to linger, though she wanted to. It wasn't the time to enjoy herself.

Finally, they turned a corner at the Harrowdel Museum of World Art, and found themselves in the cool shade of old-growth trees, grounded in an iron-fenced garden just across the street.

Petra pursed her lips. There were dozens of gardens sprawled down Arboresque Lane, where they now stood. Some were public gardens, others you had to pay a fee to view, and others still were completely private—though Petra didn't know why anyone would be so greedy as to maintain one of these lush gardens for their own eyes only.

"Let's try this way," she suggested, pointing to the right. There were more gardens down that way, and more of a chance of finding the Torrence Gardens.

"No," Evan said.

Petra furrowed her brow. "Why? Oh." She saw he was pointing to a small kiosk under the street sign, a map posted to it. It was an elaborate thing, the frame made of black wrought-iron with frilly little flourishes all down the sides.

It took seconds to locate the Torrence Gardens on the map. Petra was surprised to see even more gardens on the map than she had expected, sprawling out over several streets. Down on the First Rise, they were lucky to have a small public park nearby with trees and green grass where they could breathe in the fresh air that was so abundant up here.

"See? I was right," she said. "It's this way." And she led the way to the right again.

Evan chuckled as he followed her. "So what's the plan?"

"Try the key Monty gave us."

"And if that doesn't work?"

"Kick down the door?"

They walked on for a few steps in silence.

"Wait, you're not serious, are you?" Evan asked, and Petra didn't answer. "This is the *Guild of the Rose*. They're all over the world. The combined alchemycal knowledge of its members alone... I heard some of them can make gold out of nothing. I shudder to think of what else they can do. I don't think we should go in there guns blazing. You can't solve everything difficult with bullets, you know. Why don't we try knocking first?"

Petra frowned. "Oh, all right, I suppose; if the key doesn't work."

The Torrence Garden was one of those private gardens, with a black wrought-iron gate closed over its entrance, gilded at the top in gold. Vines trailed along the fence on either side, enough to block the view into the garden, but somehow not appearing overgrown.

The elaborate gate was locked, of course. But there was no keyhole.

Petra had to stop herself from ramming her shoulder into the gate after a stern look from Evan. Instead, she studied the wrought-iron barricade, looking for a way in, or even a bell to ring. Evan was doing the same, and the two of them poked along the fence line trying not to look like they were attempting to break in. The street was somewhat empty, the paid and public gardens having closed at sunset, their few final patrons heading home.

She walked all along both sides of the gate, and all she saw was iron and ivy. Finally she met back up with Evan at the cursed gate, hands on her hips.

"Well? Any ideas?" she demanded, flicking her long curls over her shoulder to cool her neck. She was ready to climb over the fence—or see if Evan would give her a boost, the height being too much even for her.

What terrified her was what she would do once she got inside; but she knew Jiordan was in there somewhere, and all the research in the world wouldn't tell her if he was all right or not. She had to go see him with her own eyes.

Evan pointed to the top of the gate where some words were inscribed in the gold embossed iron: *Torrence Garden, Grounded in the Elements.*

"Grounded in the elements... What does that mean?" she asked.

Evan rubbed his chin. "Hmm. Sounds like alchemy terminology to me. So this definitely *seems* like the place."

Petra stared at the words, knowing it was their only clue, their only way in. "Grounded in the *elements*," she muttered. "*Grounded* in the..." And then she looked down at the ground. She gasped.

A keyhole aligned inconspicuously with the center of the gate, set in one of the cobblestones.

She dropped to her knees, her coat furling around her as she stuffed her hand in her pocket and grabbed the gold key. The cobblestone was no ordinary stone, but perhaps metal of some kind. When she put the key in and turned it, a small click sounded in the lock, and the sound of more clicking and gears turning reverberated up through the ground.

She looked up at the gate, which swung open into the

garden.

Eleven

MAISIE

Torch lamp in hand, Maisie crept down the creaking stairs into the dark hold, back in her cherry-colored gown which had been laundered yesterday. She wasn't going to make off with one of the ship's uniforms, even though it would be more practical for what she was about to do. She was still wearing the shoes, though.

She hadn't been able to come up with any other way to get the answers she needed. Those crates with the raven symbol were going somewhere in Amaryllia that held answers about Jiordan, she was sure of it. And she was going with them.

Her morning chores in the galley were complete, finished for the voyage now that the coast of Amaryllia had been sighted at first light. She had packed up her only possession: the drawing of the tableau was firmly tucked in her bodice, wrapped in an oilcloth this time. Her Pruvian protection amulet hung from her neck. She didn't intend on jumping in the water again, but would be prepared this time at the very least.

She hadn't said goodbye to Elijah. She was hoping he would be too busy with all the confusion and chaos of docking the ship and unloading their goods before the *Aura Aqua* arrived. Her heart wrenched thinking of his boyish face and mop of curls, but she couldn't say goodbye on the ship. He had hinted at the idea of disembarking with her and showing her some of the Port of Cerise. But she wouldn't be getting off the ship with him, and she couldn't let him know what she was up to.

Besides, that ruby-eyed woman, Tria, would surely begin looking for her as soon as both ships made port. And Maisie did not want to be found.

She shone her torch lamp on the raven-stamped crates, and nearly dropped it. Elijah was sitting on the topmost one. The crowbar in her other hand slipped a fraction of an inch.

He hopped down and said, "I knew this was where you'd be as soon as they spotted the Port of Cerise."

"I—Elijah—"

"I went and looked through the backlogs of the ship's cargo, and none of them listed the crates with the raven stamp. I've seen 'em so many times, but I never thought about them before. If you need to go where they're going, I'll help you."

"W-Why?"

"Well," he paused, scuffing the damp floorboards with his foot. "You said your brother's missing right? And you're trying to find him?"

"Yes, and I think whoever he saw last has something to do with that raven symbol."

"Well, you have to go. You have to find your brother."

"But, this can't be allowed, breaking into the cargo—"

"I told you I'd help you," he said. "Why are you trying to convince me not to? You know what else isn't right? Them not listing these crates on the manifests. Two wrongs and all."

"Don't make a right."

"That's how it goes?" His face lit up in surprise, then he shrugged. "Well, I'll still help you. Come here. How were you planning on shutting yourself back in?"

Maisie paused in the motion of bringing the crowbar to the nearest crate that would hold her. "Oh, well I thought I'd just—"

"You can't just drop the lid back on, it has to be hammered shut." Elijah picked a hammer up off the ground next to some other tools he must have brought down.

"All right then."

They set to work prying the crate open, all the while hearing distant shouts above while the sailors readied to make port.

"Do you need to be up there helping? Will your father be looking for you?" Maisie asked as they finally got enough nails pried up to open it.

"Oh, no. I usually hide in my bunk until we've been docked for at least an hour. Everybody's busy, especially when the *Aura Aqua* is in our wake. If we don't unload and sell our merchandise before them, they'll get the best prices and we'll be left with nearly worthless cargo."

She poked and shifted the crate's contents, not really wanting to intrude and go through it all, but not wanting to sit on anything sharp or breakable, either. Luckily, the crate turned out to contain smaller, elegant wooden boxes, with plenty of straw padding that she could push aside and make room for herself.

He gave her a leg-up as she climbed into the crate.

"Thank you for helping me," she told him, nestling herself beside the straw and boxes. She looked into his round face and smiled. "I couldn't have figured it out without you."

"You have to come back. And tell me you found your brother." He bit his lip. "I—my older brother died along with my mother four years ago. That's why I live on the ship with Father now."

"I'm so sorry," Maisie said, reaching out to cover his hand that rested on the side of the crate. Then she smiled weakly, "I'd love to tell you when we find my brother. Maybe you could even meet him."

A grin lit up Elijah's face. "Sometimes we stay in the Port of Cerise for a few days, to give everyone a break after all the extra work of out-sailing the *Aura Aqua*—but sometimes Father has us depart in less than a day, in case they're plotting the same course again. I'm not really sure which it is this time. If you find out in time, you should come back to the ship. I'm sure Father will let you bake

 III

your way again."

She smiled back at him, hoping that would be the case.

A loud bell clanged from above, and Elijah said, "We must be about to dock! Quick, I better nail you in. And here—" he thrust a leather pouch at her. It was worn, and clinked with coins, probably all the money the boy had.

"No, I couldn't possibly—"

"Take it. Find your brother." And he lowered the lid and began hammering the nails back down.

"Thank you," she whispered, clutching the pouch in increasing darkness.

She finally stopped moving.

She was tired, and sore, and hungry. She wished she had thought to pack some of those tasteless biscuits she had been baking on the *Scarborough*. Her arms felt like jelly from bracing herself against all the movement of the crate. But it had finally stopped, for longer than just a brief respite.

The sound of men talking to one another in the echoing confines of a street met her ears, and she prayed she was at her final destination. The place where she would find answers about Jiordan.

After the sounds of people faded, she waited. Longer than she would have liked, but she had to be certain that she was alone. Finally, she pulled her crowbar from the straw and began jabbing it at the edges of the crate's ceiling until a crack of light appeared. *Fresh air.* She breathed it in for a few minutes, savoring the cool air, before wedging the crowbar in the crack and levering it up and down, more difficult now from inside the box.

The light that had seeped through the crack turned out to be streetlight. It was night. She could see she was in a narrow alleyway, and the streetlight was coming from the mouth of the alley where it met up with a well-lit main street. She peered through the open crack and surveyed the alley. It looked empty.

The only weapon she had was the crowbar, though she wished she had her shotgun back at the teashop, or at the very least Evan's sleek pistol. She hadn't wanted to steal any guns from the *Scarborough*, though, not that she had seen many. Elijah had done her enough favors, and if she were to beg a return trip from Captain Ardmore, stealing a pistol would surely put *her* in the man's crosshairs.

The crowbar would have to do. She could protect herself well enough.

Her fear of that woman Tria finding her had faded since leaving the *Scarborough*; there was no possible way the woman would know Maisie had snuck off the boat in a crate, and if she guessed as much, there were hundreds of crates in that hold, many of which would have been sold before the *Aura Aqua* had even docked. She was safe enough from Tria for now.

But whoever—or whatever—was connected to the raven was a mystery. If she was right about Jiordan's carving, the raven symbol meant a true friend. If she was wrong, well, she had just broken into their cargo and hitched a ride to their lodging or headquarters.

She wrenched the crate's lid off enough to get out, and quickly leapt out, careful of the hanging nails, crowbar in hand. Her gaze darted around the alleyway, but it was still empty, and so was the main street ahead.

She looked back at the crate and grimaced. It was obvious it had been broken into, but she didn't have a hammer, nor the time to try and make it right. She searched about the wagon the crate was sitting in and found a piece of canvas. She pulled it over the top of her crate as much as she could. It wouldn't reach all the way, stuck under some other crates as it was, but it would have to do.

She slunk around the other side of the wagon and into the shadows as she heard voices inside the building beside her. She couldn't make anything out, but as she hunched there in the dark, she studied the side of the building. There was a service entrance, which the wagon was waiting outside of. The smell of old ale and even older food came from a refuse bin nearby, telling her this was no house, but likely a tavern.

Perfect! I'll just go around to the front and ask if anyone's seen Jiordan, she thought. Then she looked down at the crowbar in her hand. It was too big for her skirt pockets, and there was no way it would fit in her bodice. She would have to abandon it, her only weapon. Well, she had been weaponless before, and she was getting used to it.

With no windows to check her reflection, she tried to fix her hair as best she could, combing through it for any straw and tucking away strays. She hoped she didn't look like she had just spent the last several hours in a crate.

She slid the crowbar into the wagon as she crept around it, heading for the mouth of the alley. As she reached the corner, she turned left, but the door to the tavern was further down. An elaborate wooden portico marked the entrance, with a black painted sign above that read *The Uncanny Raven*. And there was a clear symbol of the same raven, the jewel in its mouth a deep blue.

This was it.

She strode toward the portico but a hand on her shoulder pulled her around. She reached out an empty hand, but it was met with a man's hand the size of a dinner plate. He caught her other hand as she swung it toward his face, her nails going for his eyes but missing by an inch.

"Come on," the man grunted, yanking both of her hands behind her back now.

She was almost relieved when the man dragged her to the portico of the Uncanny Raven. For a second, she had thought it might have been the ruby-eyed witch's goon, the man who apparently captained the *Aura Aqua*.

Warm electric lamp light spilled out from the tavern as the man kicked the door open and thrust her inside, releasing her. He swung a heavy wooden bolt over the door, and she jumped.

She backed up, managing to glance at the interior of

the tavern—for it was definitely a tavern, with a long brass and wood bar, a few tables ensconced in their own alcoves lit with warm light—and it was empty.

"Who are you?" she demanded.

The older man scoffed. His grey hair was oiled back, and he had a thick grey moustache and beard, unlike any Harrowdellian man. He had a slight limp, which she noticed as he hobbled over to the rifle mounted over the bar.

"I'd like to know the same," he growled. He didn't point the rifle at her, but from the way he was holding it, she could tell he didn't need to. He could aim it in a second.

She crossed her arms. "You first."

His moustache twitched in either irritation or amusement. "Very well, missy, even though I know for a fact you broke into my crate out back."

Her cheeks grew warm, but she refused to look guilty or admit it. She tightened her arms over her chest and gave him a pointed look.

"Name's Sterling Johannsen. This is the Uncanny Raven. I think that's all you need to know."

"Actually, I don't think so—"

"—and you are?"

She hesitated. He didn't seem to want to shoot her, and if she was right about the carving, he *should* be trustworthy. But she didn't know for sure. "Maisie."

"Oh, aye? And what are you doing here, Miss Maisie?"

"Looking for something," she said guardedly.

"And you didn't find it in my crate out back, then, did you?"

"I didn't touch a thing in your crate!"

"Just browsing through it, then? Nothing to your liking?"

She huffed impatiently. She was getting nowhere with this man. Her stomach twisted as she made a decision. She just hoped it was the right one. Reaching into her bodice, she pulled out her drawing. She folded it so the raven in the corner was most visible, but not the rest of the drawing. "What do you know about this raven?" she asked quietly.

Sterling's eyes narrowed, studying the rough drawing of the raven with the stone in its mouth, then his gaze traveled to the peacock he could still see despite her folding it in quarters. He snatched the drawing out of her hands.

"Hey!" she cried, but he was already unfolding it.

His mouth curved into a grin. "Ah, so you're here to pick up Jiordan's mirror."

Twelve

PETRA

She exchanged a look with Evan, and they walked inside the open gate of the private garden side by side. The mechanical gate shut behind them in a grinding of gears, clicking shut with a resounding finality, closing them in. Petra tucked the golden key back in her coat pocket as she glanced over her shoulder.

It felt like they had stepped into a fairytale forest. Beautifully groomed decorative trees grew all around them across a neatly-manicured lawn. Statues peered at them from beside miniature shrubs.

Evan bumped into her. "Ah!" he yelped, pointing.

Petra looked. She took a step to the side as well. "It looks like it's supposed to be an angel," she said, uncertain.

"A terrifying angel," Evan replied, steering them faster down the narrow stone path.

They walked on for several minutes in silence, occasionally spotting another strange statue—once a bear with the head of a cow—and they heard the tinkling of water somewhere, but Petra had yet to see any.

"How big do you think this place is?" she wondered, growing nervous as they rounded another bend in the path. "Where is the actual headquarters?"

Evan shrugged, then stopped in his tracks. "Well, maybe he can tell us," he said under his breath.

A man stood before a fountain, bald, with a black rose pinned to his dark red overcoat, embroidered with a floral design in black. Petra didn't know what she had expected—strange robes of some kind, a funny hat maybe, but this gentleman looked perfectly normal, though a bit extravagant with the embroidered overcoat and rose.

Petra fought the urge to stop walking; instead, she approached the man as if she weren't trespassing in a private garden owned by a secret organization. "Excuse me, can you help us—"

"Right this way Miss Everturn, Mr. Rosslyn," he said, bowing his head and sweeping his arm to his right.

Her boots caught on the stone walk. She glanced at Evan. He knew who they were.

Evan shrugged slightly and cocked his head, indicating they should follow. Petra agreed, but now she was more on edge than their simple matter of trespassing. They had been expecting her. Had they been watching her?

The man in the dark red overcoat smiled politely at their acceptance and nodded. He turned to go around the fountain, which Petra could now see was a strange compilation of orbs on different tiers that actually rotated around the center column, moved by the flowing water. She thought the orbs might be planets, but couldn't be sure.

They followed the man down the cobblestone path, but they didn't go far. A modest two-story building sprung up as they crested a small hill, though it did have an impressive doorway. The two columns on either side of the simple wooden door were carved stone, meeting in an archway above. The archway was carved with several symbols Petra couldn't quite make out, but one she recognized immediately: the rose with the ray of thorns.

Evan was staring at the archway, too, and Petra had to tug on his arm as the man went to the door and held open one side for them. She was practically dragging Evan along now, and she recognized the fear in his eyes. She knew it was fear, because below her own anger that fueled her—anger at Jiordan for unearthing this Mirror, anger at the Guild for taking Maisie and Jiordan—was a pool of fear that she worked hard to keep from bubbling over.

They were meddling in things they shouldn't. The Guild of the Rose was not some book club that met every other Wednesday. They were a global organization of alchemysts. They employed people like that witch with her terrifying ruby eye—who knew what else they were capable of?

But she had to press on. Who else would? Her brother and sister needed her help. She felt a twinge of fondness for Evan for coming even this far with her. It wasn't as if his own family were in trouble. She squeezed his arm gently and they entered the headquarters of the Guild of the Rose.

The inside was dimly lit by small gas lamps along the walls, which were paneled in dark wood and red wallpaper. The floor drew her attention immediately—black and white checkered ceramic with a mesmerizing floral design on each tile. They were in an entrance hall of some kind, with nothing but a simple—yet elegant—wooden desk across from the doors. A vase of black roses was the only thing atop the desk.

"This way, please," the man said, leading them to the left and down a similarly decorated hallway. Alcoves they passed contained treasures and artifacts, reminding Petra of the tea shop. A vase of gold-wrought roses. A painting of three monks, with a black ribbon draped over one side of the frame. A collection of empty ancient-looking vials and jars.

The man stopped at the first door they encountered, on the right. It was a set of double doors, which he opened for them and gestured that they go in first. Petra shifted her shoulders, feeling the weight of her pistols in their shoulder straps hidden under her coat. Despite the unnerving feeling that they had been expected, this was going fairly well so far. Maybe they could talk their way out of this, get Jiordan and Maisie, and all go home.

Yeah, sure, she thought.

Inside the room was a library, though perhaps it was more of a study, with enough bookshelves lining the walls to give the Guild plenty of reading material, but nothing to rival Harrowdel's great libraries. A cluster of red velvet chairs nearest the door huddled beside a crackling fireplace. Two of the chairs were occupied, and Petra didn't recognize either person sitting there. Her heart fell. She had almost expected to see Jiordan or Maisie waiting for her, after all these pleasantries.

The man who led them there excused himself and left, leaving Petra and Evan standing in the open doorway. One of the room's occupants stood, a man with short black hair and thick eyebrows; he wore a deep red robe that wouldn't look out of place at a scholar's society or university. The other person remained seated, an old woman also wearing one of the scholarly robes. Her almost white hair was piled atop her head and crowned with one of those tiny decorative hats Petra detested.

"Ah, Miss Everturn, we've been expecting you," the man said, gesturing to invite them further into the study to sit down.

"I can see that," she said, unable to keep the sour note from her tone. "And who might you be?"

He bowed, exposing a slight balding at the crown of his head. "I am Sir Anton Georgoff, but you may call me Anton. And this is Madam Malavia."

The madam nodded but said nothing, surveying them through spectacles perched on her nose.

"I'm here for my brother and sister," Petra said, her hands on her hips.

Anton chuckled. "To the point, as I am told you often are. Please, come in, sit down."

Neither Petra nor Evan moved to sit down in the chairs, so Anton remained standing, his back to the fire. He clasped his hands before him, smiling. "Very well. May I offer you some tea or other refreshment? The walk through the garden is not short, I know very well."

"We're fine," Petra grumbled, grinding her boot heel into the carpet, wishing it were this smug man's face. "Jiordan and Maisie. You have them. I want them back."

At this Anton frowned. "I'm afraid I cannot give them to you."

Petra drew herself up to her fullest height and marched straight toward the man, with no idea what she was going to do to him—

"—For one thing, your sister is not here."

She stopped in her tracks. "What do you mean? She was taken on the Third Rise right near your headquarters—or, your other quarters, whatever they are."

"I can assure you, no one here has so much as spoken to your sister Maisie."

"But that woman, with the ruby eye—"

The woman sitting by the fire, Madam Malavia, made a sudden movement, as if to stand, her eyes flashing.

Anton clasped his hands behind his back. "Ah. Mistress Tria. She is... no longer a member of our Guild."

"What do you mean?" Petra barked. "She came and stole Jiordan's trunk right out of our shop! If you didn't take Maisie, then, did she?"

"I'm afraid I don't know precisely what might have

occurred. You have my deepest sympathies for your missing sister. However, I will tell you that your brother is indeed in our custody. But we cannot release him to you."

Evan intercepted Petra's reach for her pistol, grabbing her arm and pulling her close to him.

"Can you tell us why?" Evan asked Anton, giving Petra a look. "Jiordan is a free man, he has done nothing illegal."

"On the contrary," Anton replied, his eyebrows furrowing. "He has stolen a highly dangerous artifact from the Guild, and is to be indicted by the magistrate's courts of Harrowdel once the scribes in Amaryllia send the transcript of his confession."

Petra's mouth opened, but she couldn't speak. The courts of Harrowdel? How was that possible? She had thought the Guild was holding him illegally, but...

"How come he isn't in the magistrate's jail?" Evan asked, thinking along the same lines. "How can you be allowed to imprison him here?"

Anton brought his fingers together, "Ah, well, since the stolen artifact in question was a highly dangerous piece of alchemy, the magistrate has agreed that we—I should say, the Guild, is more equipped to hold him. I have the papers if you wish to see them." He vaguely indicated a desk along the side wall.

"But he didn't steal anything dangerous!" Petra said. "It's just some crackpot mirror you alchemysts want to pretend can transport a person to another place! How is that dangerous?"

Anton glanced back at Madam Malavia, who frowned

but still said nothing.

Anton went on. "I'm afraid you don't know the truth about the Mirror. What you have heard is wrong. It *is* highly dangerous. Not being Guild members, I cannot share the inner secrets of our order with you, but the outcomes—that is to say, the results of our experiments and inventions—are common enough knowledge.

"The reason the Mirror is dangerous... is that it does not do what you say it does, Miss Everturn. The Mirror is the reason Mistress Tria is no longer a Guild member. She created it. And the Mirror doesn't transport people; it kills them."

Thirteen

MAISIE

Maisie lifted her skirt as she followed Sterling down the narrow staircase into the basement of the Uncanny Raven. "Well, I was looking for Jiordan, actually," she told him. "But if the Mirror is here, maybe I can take it back to Harrowdel for him."

"His arrest by the Guild of the Rose was unfortunate. I only heard about it when they took him from the ship back to Harrowdel. It was then that I sent the trunk."

"*You* sent the trunk?" she said, halting in her steps.

"Yes, Mr. Everturn instructed that I should do so in the event of his arrest, disappearance, or actual death." Sterling reached the bottom of the steps and Maisie hustled after him.

"So what's inside the trunk, then? We could never get it open."

Sterling chuckled, lifting the small oil lamp he was carrying and placing it on a nearby crate. His beard and moustache cast strange shadows on his face in the flickering light. "It's empty."

"Empty?" Maisie started laughing now.

"The message was the carved tableau. Hidden in plain sight. And he had hoped you and your sister would recall the tale of the *Sapphire Lion* you all read together as children, and come looking here for answers." He busied himself studying the wooden floor of the basement, looking for something. "Ah," he said, dusting off a small patch of floor. He withdrew a crowbar from under his arm—Maisie suspected it was the same crowbar she had left in the wagon outside—and began prying up what appeared to be a secret hatch. It opened with a groan and fell against the floor with a bang.

"After me, I think," Sterling said, retrieving his lantern and finding his footing on a ladder in the dark hole.

Maisie waited until he had reached the bottom—she was wearing a dress for crumpet's sake—before she started descending. She wondered if she should add some outfits to her wardrobe like the sailor's uniform. She was starting to miss the freedom of trousers in an odd way. No wonder Petra favored them. Normally Maisie adored pretty dresses and skirts, but they weren't practical for stowing away in crates and climbing down ladders. Not that this was something she planned to do often.

She reached the bottom and looked around. It wasn't at all what she had expected after the dusty and cobweb-filled basement above.

Sterling had lit several gas lamps already, revealing

what appeared to be a cozy meeting room of some kind. A few tables and chairs were scattered about, mis-matched, though some looked quite expensive. Gilt-framed paintings lined the blue and gold wallpapered walls, and a few low bookshelves ran along the bottom of each wall. She even spotted a kettle and tea tins in one corner.

Sterling was fiddling with a brick beside a decorative fireplace. She could tell it was unused because inside the hearth was pristine white tile. She supposed sound could carry up through a working chimney to the main tavern if it were a real fireplace.

"Here we are," he said, pulling a velvet box from a compartment behind the brick he had removed.

"What is this place?" Maisie wondered. A secret compartment in a secret meeting room, hiding Jiordan's treasure.

Sterling hesitated for a moment, then his moustache twitched and he said, "This is a meeting house of the International and Ancient Order of Branwen."

"The... what?" *Not another secret society*, she thought.

"The Order of Branwen, we call it for short."

"And Jiordan is a member?"

"Indeed," Sterling said, nodding once. "Along with your father and mother. Under normal circumstances, I would not divulge this information to you, but the Everturns have always been one of our prominent families. And Jiordan's situation with the Guild of the Rose, and this Mirror, has given flight to all manner of unexpected circumstances."

He extended the black velvet box to her, the size of a book. She took it but didn't open it yet. The mention of her parents knowing about—and being members of—this order pushed all thoughts of the Mirror aside.

"What do you mean?"

"Well, firstly, the Guild has begun to extend its reach into our affairs, which is unprecedented." He shook his head. "The Order of Branwen existed long before those alchemysts came clawing out of their laboratories, with their fanciful 'discoveries'."

"But what does the Order of Branwen do, exactly?" Maisie asked.

Sterling ran a finger along the mantlepiece beside him, inspecting it for nonexistent dust. "This and that," he said mysteriously. "We are an order of people from all ways of life, and we are truth-seekers above all else. Sure, we have some alchemysts in our number, but that's not what our order was founded on."

He pointed to a large painting on the wall behind Maisie. She turned to study it. It was a somewhat abstract painting of a raven, its wings outstretched. As she edged closer to it, she realized that the raven was actually made up of smaller images: people mostly, painted in black and white so that when looked at from afar they blended into the feathers of the bird. And above the bird, a scroll was painted at the top, with the words: *Flying on the Wings of Truth.*

If both her parents and Jiordan were members, she felt she could trust Sterling and the Order. Perhaps she could even stay at the tavern until she could get back to the *Scarborough,* that is, if the ship wasn't leaving right away.

"All right," Maisie said slowly, "But what do you *do—*"

A squawk interrupted her. She turned to see a small mechanical raven in the corner of the room, which she had thought was just a statue. It squawked again.

"Hmm," Sterling said. "It appears someone is in the tavern above. Someone not of the Order." He quickly closed up the brick in the wall of the fireplace where he had taken the Mirror from, then strode across the room, darting around the chairs despite his slight limp.

"How do you—?"

"The raven. The tavern was locked. If it were someone from the Order, they would have disabled the call from alerting us. I need to talk to Monty about a new lock on that door," he said to himself. "I don't know why we're still using damned *wood* to lock it."

He was now fiddling with a painting on the back wall. "Could you have been followed? Does anyone know you're here?"

The raven squawked again.

Sterling darted over to the mechanical bird and flipped a switch at the base of the statue. Something like a thin black pipe rose from the surface behind the bird, and Sterling put his eye to the curved end.

Maisie thought back to Elijah, but he hadn't known where the raven-stamped cargo would be sent to. Then she gasped. "The ruby-eyed woman! Tria something.

From the Guild." Frantically, she glanced at the ladder leading up to the basement. It was the only way out.

"It's her," Sterling said with a nod, then flipped the switch again and the pipe disappeared back behind the raven.

She stuffed the velvet Mirror box in her oversized skirt pocket—the dress was good for that, at least—and rushed over to the ladder to peer up at the trap door which she had closed behind her on her way down.

"Not that way," Sterling hissed as he rushed back over to the painting on the far wall, a boring oil painting of a boring old man sitting in a chair.

"What way, then?" she said, turning to look for another exit she hadn't seen. "We're trapped down here. If that ruby-eyed witch catches me, she'll just use her creepy eye again, and then she'll have Jiordan's Mirror!"

"No, she won't. There's another way out, just wait a moment. Ah," he said finally, and Maisie heard a latch click.

For a wild moment she thought the painting would swing away to reveal a hidden tunnel like in books she had read, but now Sterling was bending down to push aside the low bookcase underneath the painting. He rolled it down along the wall as if it held only one book, not the hundred sitting on its dark lacquered shelves.

"Where does it go?" Maisie demanded, bending over to peer in.

Another squawk came from the mechanical bird in the corner.

She spoke again before Sterling could reply, "It doesn't matter—can I get to the harbor? If I get back on the *Scarborough,* I can hide out there until—"

"The *Scarborough*?" he asked. "They're leaving at midnight, there was a change in plans."

"But—how do you know that?"

"A message with the crates," Sterling said, reaching out for her hand and guiding her to the low opening in the wall. "Here, take this, it might help—" he stuffed a piece of cloth into her hand and she jammed it into her bodice without looking. He was helping her lower her head already into the opening. "I'd say you're an honorary member of the Order after all this."

"Aren't you coming?" she asked, lifting a tentative hand up to see how high the tunnel was. She had a few inches above her head and that was it.

"Oh no," Sterling said, running the fingers of one hand down both sides of his moustache. "I'd like to meet this woman; I've heard many a tale about her. And I can't leave the Uncanny Raven unattended. Go, the lights will ignite as you get further up into the tunnel."

"Are you su—"

"Go!" he hissed, as the mechanical raven squawked again.

And with that, he began rolling the bookcase back over the tunnel, leaving her in complete darkness.

She couldn't hear anything through the heavy bookcase, so she began to crawl down the tunnel. After only a few feet, a gas lamp flickered to life, mounted to the left wall.

"So much for staying at the tavern," she muttered to herself.

As soon as she reached the lamp, the ceiling rose up high enough for her to stand. The walls were just as decorative as the meeting room, with gold and blue wallpaper and gilt molding lining the ceiling.

She paused a moment to slow down her heartbeat. She was relatively safe in the tunnel for a time. She didn't know if Tria would even discover the hidden meeting room, but if Sterling wanted her to go out this way, so be it. She would work her way back to the harbor and find the *Scarborough*. She just hoped she got to it before they left port. And if Sterling was right, she only had until midnight.

The strange weight of the Mirror in her pocket drew her attention. She slipped out the velvet box and opened it for the first time. In the steady light of the lamp, the Mirror glinted at her, but not like a normal mirror. It was the color of a deep red wine, with facets throwing light in all directions. The surface looked entirely smooth, though. Her fingers were drawn toward it, but she stopped an inch from it.

An idea flickered through her head, and she wondered if she should try to use it. Evan had said the Mirror was supposed to transport a person to another place. Well, if it worked, she could transport herself right back to Harrowdel. Right back to the tea shop if she wanted—right?

She bit her lip and drew back her hand. She had no idea how it worked. What if she touched it and ended up on a whole different continent? Or in the middle of the ocean?

"Petra would kill me," she said aloud. "For trying in the first place."

She snapped the lid shut and stuffed the thing back in her pocket.

As she walked up the tunnel—for it began to rise on an incline—gas lamps sprung to fiery life as she approached each one. Looking back, the lights extinguished after she had gone by, too. She had to stop herself from experimenting with them, wanting to run up and down the tunnel to see what would happen. But she had to make it to the harbor before midnight.

So she kept walking. She still had no idea what time it was, she only knew that she was growing hungrier and more tired by the minute. The biscuit she had eaten before leaving the *Scarborough* seemed like decades ago. She was so hungry she was beginning to imagine the smell of baked bread. Pastries. Cakes. Her mouth was watering against her will.

But wait— *was* she imagining it? The tunnel suddenly evened out, no longer on an incline, and she didn't think she was imagining the delicious scents wafting down the tunnel; she could practically taste them. Was she at the end?

As she took a step forward, she caught sight of a door— right before the last lamp behind her extinguished, and no others lit in its place. *This must be the end,* she thought.

Carefully she crept forward, feeling for the door in the now pitch-black tunnel.

Sterling hadn't said where it let out, so she would have to be careful. She was, at least, far from the ruby-eyed witch. She wished she had a pistol. Or that crowbar, at the very least. She patted her pockets and bodice. All she had on her was the Mirror, her Pruvian necklace, the now pointless drawing of the trunk, and the scrap of fabric Sterling had handed her. Too late to figure out what it was now.

She put her hand on the doorknob, but stopped. Leaning closer, she put her ear to the solid wood, but she could hear nothing. She took a deep breath, and turned the handle.

Fourteen

PETRA

Petra slammed the door of the tea shop behind her, striding over to the counter and ripping off her coat as she went. A dull glow coming from the kitchen was the only light.

A quiet jingling told her Evan had followed her inside.

She strode behind the counter and grabbed a leftover teapot—half-full of Hazelnut Midnight—cold as ice, but she poured the contents into a large cup anyway and drank some down.

Evan sat at one of the stools at the end of the counter, fiddling with his hat.

"If they just let me *talk* to him," Petra fumed after her next sip.

"I know."

"They really can't be allowed to hold him there."

"I agree."

"Well what are we going to do?" she demanded, tired

of his short answers.

Evan placed his hat squarely in the center of the counter. "I don't know. Since they took the key, we'd really have to break in to talk to Jiordan. And if they're holding him legally, we'll be even more at risk of breaking the law."

Petra bit the inside of her lip. "I can't believe they took the key." After the nameless Guild member escorted them back through the garden, he had demanded their key, and Petra had still been in too much shock to put up an argument.

"I can believe it," Evan said. "They're probably only given to Guild members."

"Which makes me wonder why your friend Monty had one."

Evan nodded slowly. "Yes, that is curious. But he didn't know where their headquarters were—and he made us that bug to spy on them. Why would he do all that if he were a member?"

"Why indeed." Petra took another sip of her cold tea. "I'm going back there. Tonight."

"You can't," Evan said.

"Why not?" she asked recklessly. To hell with planning. Planning had gotten her nowhere all these months. She had found where Jiordan was as soon as she had started listening to Evan—and pursuing the Guild like Maisie had wanted to in the first place.

"They knew we were coming," Evan said. "These people are dangerous, Petra, remember? You could get into more trouble than just breaking the law. The Mirror killing people? Do you know what else these alchemysts could be hiding?"

"I don't care. I'll take Maisie's shotgun."

"You can't go. I won't let you." He intercepted her next reach for her teacup and grabbed her hand.

"I won't let you stop me," she retorted, snatching away her suddenly warm hand. She strode around to the front of the counter toward him. Picking up his hat, she handed it to him. "I think you should go."

"And I think you need to slow down," he said, returning his hat to the counter. "I'm not going anywhere right now."

"Why do you *care*, Evan? Why are you even here?" she demanded, rounding on him.

"Because," he said, then took both her arms and kissed her.

His warm mouth sparked against hers, lighting a path from her lips to her chest. His arms went around her, and she sank into the warmth of them, wrapped up in the smell of his citrus cologne, his strange yet soft beard, and the smooth linen of his coat.

And then she remembered who she was kissing. She backed away.

"I—why—" she sputtered.

He perched himself back on a stool and suddenly looked sheepish, covering his mouth with his hand.

Initially intent on raging at him for his audacity, she suddenly slumped against the tea counter, head in her hands and elbows propped on the counter. She wasn't even that mad at him, and she didn't have the energy. "I don't know what to do, Evan."

He made a soft happy noise and scooted the stool closer. He didn't touch her, but his closeness was somehow nice. He placed his hands on the counter near hers.

"I want to talk to Jiordan," she said. "That Sir Anton said that the Mirror kills people. Did you know about that?"

"No. I had only ever seen descriptions saying it was meant for matter transportation. What do people need another killing tool for? I just thought it was a fascinating idea that it could be used to go somewhere in an instant."

"Do you think Jiordan knew before he stole it?" she asked in a whisper.

Evan sighed. "No. The Jiordan I knew was just as excited as I was at the prospect of transportation."

She nodded. "I'd still like to talk to him."

"I think that's a good idea. But we have no way to get in there anymore."

She closed her eyes, sinking deeper into her hands. The lack of sleep from last night was catching up to her. Then she felt something at her elbow. She opened her eyes and saw that Evan had nudged her cup of cold tea beside her. She let out a reluctant chuckle and lifted her head from her hands, reaching for the cup.

"What about Monty?" she said, the drink halfway to her lips.

"What about him?"

"Well he's all we've got. He knows *something* about the Guild. Maybe he can help us again."

"Perhaps..." Evan hedged.

"He can tell us why he had that key at least."

"True. But it's late. We can't go barging in there now."

"Why not? Those transcripts for Jiordan's trial could come any time now. Who knows how quickly those creeps will push them through the courts?"

"Let's wait until tomorrow. He has a family and all."

Petra rolled her eyes. It was *her* family that was in trouble. "Fine."

"Fine? Really?"

"Yes, I suppose I should get some rest. The shop looks a mess. If I'm going to have Weston run it all day tomorrow while we go talk to Monty and hopefully Jiordan, I'll need to set it straight first thing in the morning. Besides, I'd like to count the money anyway."

He grinned at her. "I'm just impressed you're listening to me."

She punched him lightly on the shoulder. "Who says that's what I'm doing?"

"I do." He grabbed her fist and drew her in closer.

She was wrapped up in his citrus scent, sending heady waves of warmth through her. "Stop that," she whispered, however unwilling to pull away. His other hand went around the back of her neck and she shivered.

"No," he whispered back. "I think you like it. I think you don't like the idea of liking me."

"What gave you that idea?"

And there in the night dark tea shop, he kissed her again, and this time she didn't pull away.

Fifteen

MAISIE

She emerged onto a crowded street and quickly shut the tunnel door behind her. The door was inconspicuous in a small niche beside a building. The smell of baked bread and pastries was now overwhelming. It was coming from the shop to her right. Even though it was late—she was sure it was approaching midnight—the lights of the bakery glared into the busy street, welcoming customers. *How odd*, Maisie thought. *Bakeries are never open this late in Harrowdel.*

Under the scent of pastries, she could also smell the ocean. She must be close to the docks. She wanted to get back to the ship as soon as she could. She didn't want to miss its departure, and she should probably talk to the captain about letting her back on board first. If he didn't agree, she might have to sneak back on. She knew Elijah would want to help her.

She lingered by the bakery, trying to estimate which

way to the docks. Most of the traffic seemed to be flowing to and from the right side of the street, and she figured sailors were stretching their legs and their coin purses before they were confined to their ships again. She hoped she would be among those returning to their ships. She just needed to *find* the docks, and the ship.

"Maisie?" a voice called from the door of the bakery.

It was Elijah. He was holding a wax-coated paper bag, brimming with pastries and reeking of cinnamon. He had one of the cinnamon buns in his hand, and sugar dusted his lips.

Maisie smiled and edged through the crowded street.

"I'm stocking up," Elijah said, lifting the bag in indication. "Mrs. Cable makes the best cinnamon buns in the world."

She glanced into the shop, full of patrons calling out orders. "They look good," she agreed. "But you can't say they're the best in the world until you try one of mine."

"Really?"

"Well of course, if you stay in Harrowdel long enough for me to bake some. Unless your father or the quartermaster will allow me more flour and sugar on the way back. And some cinnamon."

Elijah led them away from the crowded bakery, in what appeared to be the direction of the docks. He took a huge bite out of his bun and said nothing, suddenly quiet.

"Is something wrong?" Maisie asked.

"Ah, well, I don't think I'll be in Harrowdel for another few months actually."

Maisie stopped walking and grabbed his arm. "What do you mean?"

"I heard my father talking to Mr. Garris before I left the ship. They're changing their shipping routes again. I guess even though we beat the *Aura Aqua* here, their captain sent word ahead of time and bought out all the merchants in the Port of Cerise. So we were able to sell our cargo, but have nothing to load the ship back up with. We'll have nothing to sell at the next port. We have to get them to stop tailing us."

Maisie's mouth dropped open, and it wasn't just because it was watering at the smell of the cinnamon buns. "The *Scarborough* isn't sailing back to Harrowdel?"

Elijah dug in the bag and handed her a bun, which she forced herself to eat neatly, though she wanted to rip it apart with her hands. "Not for a while anyway."

Maisie glanced at the street around her with its foreign shops, many still open for their nautical clientele. The cinnamon bun suddenly felt like sand in her mouth. She forced herself to chew through it. She would either be stuck on board the *Scarborough* for months, or she would have to stay in the Port of Cerise until another ship would accept a passenger whose only payment would be in baking skills.

She licked the cinnamon sugar off her lips as they continued walking. Perhaps she could convince the captain to make a change in the routes. Perhaps she could promise to bake a hundred cakes to supply his ship when they docked in Harrowdel.

But as Elijah pointed to the left where the busy road led to the docks, all thoughts of cakes and ships slipped from her mind.

A man with grey hair stood at the corner, leaning against a lamppost, his arms crossed. Maisie would recognize him anywhere. It was the ruby-eyed witch's accomplice. He had been there, robbing their shop, trespassing into Maisie and Petra's bedroom to steal Jiordan's trunk. And now he was here.

He pushed himself off the lamppost and strode toward her. Maisie instinctively stepped back, bumping into Elijah.

"Huh," Elijah said. "What's he doing here?"

"You know him?" Maisie asked, wanting to run away but she was so close to Elijah and the rest of the pedestrians she couldn't go anywhere.

"That's the captain of the *Aura Aqua*. That crook."

That's right. But was the ruby-eyed witch here by the port, too? Or was she still back at the Uncanny Raven, searching for Maisie? It didn't matter; the man was closing in on them.

To her surprise, Elijah stepped in front of her. He shoved the bag of pastries into Maisie's arms.

It surprised the captain, too. He paused right in front of them, evaluating.

Maisie tried to study him in the light of the flickering gas streetlamps. His grey hair was cut fashionably short, and he had an expensive mauve suit on, complete with a black and gold cravat at his throat.

"Out of our way," Elijah said, throwing his chest out.

"It's a public street, little captain," the man replied. His voice wasn't as smooth as Maisie thought it would be. It was coarse, as if he were only pretending to be wealthy and mysterious. It sounded like he had grown up on the Low Rise of Harrowdel.

"And you're blocking it," Elijah replied.

"That's because I want to talk to your friend, here."

Maisie looked away for a moment, growing uncomfortable under the older man's gaze. She stared at the pastries in her arms for a second then looked back up. Surely he wouldn't do anything as rash as try to kidnap her in the middle of a crowded street? She didn't want Elijah getting hurt, either.

She tried to force her way in front of Elijah, but he conceded by standing at her side. She gave him a small smile before glancing back at the captain in distaste. "I don't believe we've been introduced. Now, if you'll excuse us, we must be going—"

He reached out and grabbed her arm. The bag of pastries tumbled to the ground in a cinnamon sugar mess. Maisie reached out with her other arm and tried to pry him off. She had *had it* with strangers grabbing her.

Elijah tried to jump into the fray, but Maisie held him back.

"No, Elijah, stay back. I can handle this!"

She couldn't pry the man's hand off, and now he was fumbling inside his breast pocket for something. Maisie's heartbeat slammed against her ribcage. A gun? A knife?

Would he force her back to his ship?

But he pulled out a monocle. A red, glittering monocle, exactly like whatever made up Tria's disturbing eye.

He put it to his eye, and for a second Maisie felt weak at the knees. *No!* she thought, feeling Elijah beside her slump to the ground.

The edges of her vision grew red, but the effect wasn't overtaking her fully like it had before. The captain's grip on her arm became painful, his fingers digging into her skin as if trying to force the gem's power upon her.

But it wasn't working. In fact, the red at the edge of her vision was clearing, and a sudden warmth radiated from her chest, as if fighting off the ill-effects of the monocle. And then she remembered. The Pruvian amulet! She yanked the black crystal necklace out of her bodice. The captain stumbled backward, dropping his monocle on the ground, breaking into pieces.

"Curses," he cried, fumbling on the ground for the pieces. "Tria is going to *kill* me."

Elijah had fallen on the ground, unconscious from the gem's full power over him, his brown curly hair falling in his eyes. She rushed to lift his head and shoulders, wanting to get as far away from the *Aura Aqua's* captain as fast as possible.

She hefted Elijah up and dragged him a few steps away from the captain, wondering how such a small boy could possibly be so heavy. Then she felt a hand on her shoulder.

She shuddered. *No, not the ruby-eyed witch.*

But when she turned, she was faced with a different

menacing face entirely.

"What's wrong with the boy?" quartermaster Garris demanded.

Never in her life had she thought she would be relieved to see this man. "He was attacked by that man back there," she told him, pointing.

They watched the captain of the *Aura Aqua*, still scrounging on the ground for shards of the evidently-priceless ruby-like material.

"Right, well, come on then." Garris grabbed hold of one of Elijah's arms, and they carried him between them, the tips of the boy's toes bumping across the cobblestoned street as they made a beeline to the docks.

The *Scarborough* wasn't far. Garris hoisted Elijah onto his shoulder and headed up the gangplank. Maisie followed, watching the night-dark water below her as she tiptoed up the creaking boards.

"What happened?" Captain Ardmore demanded, striding over to them as soon as they set foot on the ship.

Garris laid down Elijah amid a bed of coiled rope. "I was going to collect the boy from the bakery like you asked, when I came across him like this. The girl says Captain Phillip did it."

Captain Ardmore drew a sharp breath and shared an indeterminable look with Mr. Garris.

The gaze with which Captain Ardmore then leveled upon Maisie made her stop breathing. "Tell me," he said, his deep baritone penetrating her very bones.

She explained everything that had happened between

meeting up with Elijah outside of the bakery and their rescue by Mr. Garris. There was no need to tell him where she was before the bakery, or how and when she had left the ship, even.

"The amulet," Captain Ardmore said when she had finished, "may I see it?"

She pulled it out of her bodice again, where she had tucked it after Garris had come upon them. The piece of cloth Sterling had given her dislodged and fell to the deck. The captain picked it up and stared at it. It appeared to be a handkerchief, with some kind of design on one corner, but she couldn't see it from where she stood.

After a moment, he folded it up and handed it back to her, saying nothing.

"The amulet?"

"Oh, right." She pulled it over her head and handed it over.

"Pruvian, you said?"

She nodded. "My father's."

"Very well," the captain said, handing the amulet back to her and glancing at the handkerchief in her hands.

Maisie's thoughts whirled. Perhaps Phillip's monocle didn't have the full power Tria's ruby eye did, or perhaps the protection amulet really *did* work. She thought back to when Tria tried to take her, wondering if that was why she hadn't fallen under the ruby's power as completely as the first time.

"Miss Everturn," the captain said. "If you would be so kind as to meet me in my quarters? And Mr. Garris, tell the crew to take us underway as soon as we're cleared with the harbormaster."

He picked up his son and Maisie followed him to the sturdy door that led to the captain's quarters.

As she followed, she opened the handkerchief with shaking hands. On the bottom right corner was embroidered the raven of the Order of Branwen.

After seeing his son settled into one of the neat bunks tucked in an alcove off the main room, Captain Ardmore sat down behind an enormous wooden desk that looked as if it would survive a shipwreck if it ever came to one.

"Please, sit," he said, pointing to the two worn paisley upholstered chairs before the desk.

The quarters were neat and tidy, with one wall of shelves containing what looked like ledgers, and a fair smattering of novels. There was a sturdy round table and chairs, and a painting hung behind the door of a beautiful woman with long chestnut hair, and a boy who looked almost like Elijah. Few other personal items took up any room, however. The room was all business, just like the captain.

Maisie clutched at the handkerchief as she lowered herself into one of the chairs, glancing at the captain. He seemed too calm for someone whose son had just been brought to the ship unconscious, attacked by his rival.

But he had said they would be underway soon, she thought. *So he wasn't going to kick her off the ship, right?*

"He should be fine," Maisie blurted. "Elijah. He should wake up in a few hours."

The captain nodded and stared for a long while at the bunk where Elijah lay. Then finally, he said, "Miss Everturn, I wasn't aware you were a member of the Order of Branwen."

She exhaled in relief. "Oh, that," she said, finally leaning back in the chair. "Well, I'm new, I guess." Sterling *did* say she was an honorary member.

The captain pulled open a desk drawer and drew out a pistol.

Maisie stiffened. Had she said the wrong thing? Was the captain at odds with the Order?

But he placed it on the desk in front of her and slid it closer, so she could see the raven engraved along the handle, a sapphire in its mouth—a real gem set in the metal.

Her mouth popped open in understanding. She leaned back in the chair again, her exhaustion finally catching up to her.

"Just what did happen with Captain Phillip?" he asked, stowing his pistol again.

"It was like I told you. Phillip stunned him with the monocle, but I had the amulet, so I think it protected me. But what I didn't tell you—is I've encountered him before."

He leaned back and crossed his arms, his silence

inviting her to continue.

She told him all about how Jiordan went missing, the trunk, and the ruby-eyed witch's pursuit of her. Then she bit her lip and looked down at her borrowed shoes as she told him how she got off the ship and found her way to the Uncanny Raven to meet Sterling.

To her surprise, the captain burst out in deep guffaws.

"We wondered where you had got to," he said. "Garris joked that you could have snuck off in a crate, but never did I think..." He laughed again. "I'll have to buy him a drink at the next port for guessing that."

Maisie felt herself smiling, her cheeks still warm from the admission.

"So you're Jiordan's sister," he said.

She nodded. "It seems like everyone knows him."

"He's booked passage with me once or twice over the years, but I've never met with him on land. I don't get to too many meetings, but I do some important work for the Order here and there," he said vaguely.

Maisie finally folded up the raven handkerchief. "Well, the Guild of the Rose is holding Jiordan, Sterling told me. For stealing something from them I guess." She absently ran her hand across where the Mirror sat in her dress pocket.

"Aye, I've heard all about it. The Order has been doing their best to intercept the papers the Guild needs to indict Jiordan."

"Really? How do you—?"

Captain Ardmore winked at her. "I do some work for

the Order, remember?"

"Captain," she said abruptly. "Is it possible to head back to Harrowdel? I think I might be able to free Jiordan from the Guild."

"Not without those papers, you won't," he said. "And you can call me August."

"But how can I get the papers? What are they?"

"The Guild says they obtained a confession from Jiordan for stealing the Mirror—yes, I know what it is— and that the Amaryllian notary witnessed it. But the Order knows that's false. In truth, those sneaking alchemysts hired a skilled forger in Amaryllia to send the documents. But unfortunately for the Guild, the papers keep going missing."

Maisie grinned. "Really? How?"

"A friend I know in the Harrowdel port. The Order protects its true friends."

Just then, a knock came at the door, and Mr. Garris entered.

"We're lifting the anchor, Captain," he announced.

August stood and ran a hand down his lapels. "Garris, alert the crew: I'm changing the routes again. I believe we need to make that return trip to Harrowdel after all."

Sixteen

PETRA

It was mid-afternoon before Petra could get away from the tea shop. Weston had done fairly well closing it by himself yesterday, but for some reason today he didn't seem so confident. Twice he poured the wrong temperature water in pots to steep—"The burners are labeled for crumpet's sake," Petra had muttered—and once he almost knocked over the large jar of biscotti on the counter, but she had caught it just in time.

Finally, around three o'clock she gave up babysitting Weston and collected Evan from his corner seat where he had sat nursing a pot of Gunpowder Orange tea all day. They left Weston and the shop to their own fates.

"I can come back for closing if we don't get anywhere with Monty," Petra said to Evan as they left Cordial Crescent. "I don't know what happened with Weston, he seemed perfectly capable when I was training him."

Evan shrugged. "Maybe he lost his confidence after

being alone yesterday."

Petra rolled her eyes to herself. "I don't know. Maybe."

Then she felt something touch her hand, and Evan's fingers slipped into hers. A jolt ran up her whole arm, sparking at her fingertips. A smile flitted to her lips but then she dropped the corners of her mouth down, along with Evan's hand. He said nothing. As much as she liked his attentions—she reluctantly admitted to herself—now was not the time. They needed to figure out a way to get back into the Guild and talk to Jiordan.

Monty's shop was closed, so they pulled the bell and went around to the back door. Evan didn't seem to think it strange that the inventor had closed up while the street was still full of people doing their shopping, but Petra did. So when no one answered the pull of the bell, she was hardly surprised.

"Maybe he's gone out," Evan said.

"I don't know," Petra replied slowly, glancing around. She was tall enough to see through the small glass pane at the top of the door, so she put both hands on it to see through the darkness inside.

The workshop was in ruins. Gadgets, tools, and gears were strewn about on the floor, knocked off tables and pulled from shelves. Ceramic pots had been smashed; their plants left helpless in the shards.

Petra gasped. "It's been ransacked."

"No," Evan said, arching up on his tiptoes to gaze inside.

"A robbery? Or do you think the Guild did this?" she asked. She couldn't tell what—if anything—had been taken. It had looked nearly as messy the time she had been inside, but with a kind of controlled chaos. This was destruction.

"No one would rob Montgomery Hartford," Evan said.

"Just like no one would rob the Everturns," Petra muttered. "It had to be them."

Evan pulled Petra back down the busy street. "Let's go, we might not want to be here."

Petra followed but wasn't sure she agreed. "Shouldn't we report this to the magistrate's men?"

Evan shook his head and led her down a different street than the one they had walked down to get here. "If the Guild's involved, the magistrate might not do anything. The way they're letting them handle Jiordan's trial and all. I wonder if they have a member on the magistrate's court? That would explain the odd influence..." he spoke as if to himself, in a rambling sort of way.

Petra was only half listening. "We should get back to the tea shop," she said, a sudden worry growing in the pit of her stomach.

"No," Evan said, reaching out and taking hold of her hand.

Petra shook him off. "Why not? If the Guild thinks

they can get away with doing *that* to my family's shop, they've got another thing coming."

"No," he said again, but softer. He pulled her to the side of the street. "We don't even know what the Guild might have done to Monty. They clearly have resources deep within Harrowdel and the magistrate's. It's too dangerous to go back now. What if they imprisoned Monty, too, for helping us? What if they arrest us both? All on some charge related to interfering with Jiordan's case?"

Petra opened her mouth several times to respond. "Y-You really think they would do that?"

"I wouldn't put it past them."

"But the shop—Weston—"

"I'm sure Weston will be fine. He did all right yesterday. And the shop was in one piece an hour ago—I bet they wouldn't do something to it in the middle of the day. Monty's place could have been hit last night for all we know."

"Then let's go back, lock everything up, I'll get the shotgun—"

"They would be fools not to be watching the shop. They probably have someone there watching you—watching us. It's too risky."

"Then where do you suggest we go?" she asked tartly, tired of him shutting down everything she said.

He shrugged. "The inn where I'm staying. I doubt they'd spare a lackey to spy down there on the Low Rise."

Petra crossed her arms. "And why should we go there?

Why not just go back to the Guild?"

"Well, we didn't get answers from Monty. I thought we had agreed not to storm the place."

"Yes, but—"

"—And don't you remember what happened when we went up to the Sixth Rise yesterday, at the lifts?"

"So?"

"So, I'm wondering if that was the Guild trying to slow us down from reaching the Sixth Rise. If they have influence over the lifts..." he arched his eyebrows at her.

"They couldn't stop us from going up there."

He shook his head sadly. "It seems like they might. We need to make a better plan, and we'll need to stop and gather more information somehow." He reached out to take her hand, but she pulled away.

"Fine," she said. "Let's go to the inn then. I'm just glad I have my pistols on me."

Petra was silent the entire walk as they passed down each rise, then got into the massive lifts leading down to the Low Rise. A crowd of people pressed in beside them as the lift doors clanged shut, and Petra was forced into Evan. He put his hands on her arms and she blushed, unable to move away even if she could. But she didn't know why she wanted to.

He was nice. And clever. Far more intelligent than any of the few gentlemen she had briefly dated in the recent years. There was the fact that he had held a gun to her the first time they had met, but she didn't really fault him for it. He had just been trying to get help to find Jiordan, which was fairly touching when she thought about it, even if he did go about it the wrong way at first.

So why was she so hesitant about Evan? Perhaps she was tired of all the explorers in her life. Did she really want to get involved with another one? To only have him go missing on an expedition like her father, like her brother? To have him always chasing down some artifact, some relic?

Or was it only that now wasn't the time to be thinking selfishly of herself? She did like Evan. But shouldn't she be concentrating on helping Jiordan? Then a small voice at the back of her head made her wonder: Why couldn't she be happy in the meantime as well? For a brief moment she leaned forward and rested her forehead on his shoulder, eyes closed. The tension at the back of her neck eased momentarily.

The lift reached the bottom and she lifted her head. She still didn't know what to do about Evan. She shrugged as the lift began emptying, and she felt for her pistols in their shoulder straps. *Now's not the time for this*, she thought to herself. She could think about what might happen between her and Evan *after* they had rescued Jiordan.

She kept her eye out on the way to the Boxton Inn, letting Evan lead the way. She wanted to make sure they weren't being followed. The Low Rise was full of bustling activity in the mid-afternoon, as it always was with the proximity of the docks. The scent of the ocean wasn't overpowering enough to wash out the scent of gear grease and steam of the dozens of lifts at their backs, or the musty smell that always seemed to linger on the dingy streets that were never cleaned except when it rained. No one followed them.

As soon as they stepped into the inn, Petra paused. Were they to hole up in Evan's room together? For how long? She hadn't thought about that until now. She should see if they had another room she could rent. Thankfully, she had her billfold in her coat, just in case.

As the keeper of the tavern approached them at the door, Petra's worry about sharing a room subsided. Past the tavern keeper, she could see the obvious figure of Montgomery J. Hartford sitting in the back parlor, his black spectacles flashing in the light of the afternoon sun coming in the windows.

"Mr. Rosslyn," the tavern keeper said. "You have a guest."

"I see that," Evan said slowly.

"Would you like some tea, or—"

"Nothing, please," Evan interrupted. "Just the parlor."

"Very well."

Once the parlor door was shut behind them, Petra turned to demand information from Monty, but then held her tongue. The inventor was shaken. The hair under his bowler cap was askew, and his black traveling coat was covered in dust. His hands, sitting on the table, were a knot of fingers that kept tangling and untangling.

"What happened?" Evan asked gently. "We saw the workshop."

"The Guild of the Rose is what happened, I think you

know very well. You two are in big trouble. Do you have any idea who you're dealing with?"

"Not really," Petra admitted. Then she bit her lip and soldiered on. "We were kind of hoping you could tell us more about them."

"More? More? Oh, sure, all they have left to take from me is just my wife. Don't worry about us."

Petra exchanged horrified looks with Evan. "Your wife," she said. "Is she all right?"

"She is for now. But I didn't want her to know about any of this Guild business. And now our shop and our home is a wreck. What do I tell her, eh? Should have never given you that blasted key."

"I'm so sorry," Evan said. "We didn't know we were putting you in such a precarious position."

"Er—" Petra began. "Why did you have that key, anyway?"

Monty grunted and settled further into the hardback wooden chair, his arms crossed. "It was given to me. A long time ago. Before I knew better how to choose who I invented for." He paused, massaging the bridge of his nose underneath where the black spectacles perched.

"The Guild hired me to create a lot of things for them back then, when I was first starting out. The money was good, and I was an idiot. I was courting Adora at the time, and I never thought she would have me, a poor, blind inventor. But I thought, with the Guild's money, I wouldn't be poor anymore. I could open up my own shop and create a life for us. I'm still not sure if it was ever worth it. Adora would have had me whether I wore rags and slept on the street—apparently—I just didn't know it at the time."

"So the Guild just *gave* you the key?" Evan asked.

Monty nodded. "Aye, as a thank-you for the work I did; they said I was always welcome to join them. I never gave them an answer in return. Until yesterday, that is; when they saw you with my key, I think they took it as a definite no."

"But why did you give it to us?" Petra asked. "If it would get you into trouble?"

The old inventor shrugged. "I didn't know how the Guild would react. I run with a better crowd now. I should have prepared something for intruders at the shop. Ah well, next time."

"Do you want me to call for some food? Tea?" Evan asked.

"No, I'll be out of here soon. I just wanted to try and talk to you before Adora and I leave is all."

"Leave?" Petra said. "Where are you going?"

"I've booked passage for me and Adora on a merchant ship to Amaryllia. Going to see some old friends there until all this Guild business blows over."

Petra glanced at Evan, meeting his gaze. She wanted to ask Monty more, but they had already caused the inventor so much trouble.

Evan nodded and spoke, "Monty... I know we've put you through a lot. But is there any way you could tell us more about the Guild headquarters on the Sixth Rise?

Have you ever been there?"

Monty didn't speak for a moment, then took a deep breath. "You're still going through with this then? After what they did to my shop? That could be yours next," he directed at Petra.

She swallowed. "I know," she said softly. "But they are holding my brother prisoner. They admitted that they have him. And I don't think he's going to get a fair trial behind those closed gates when they get all the paperwork they need."

Monty grunted. "They have your brother?"

Petra nodded, forgot he couldn't see it, then said, "Yes."

"And what did he do to entice their wrath? No, wait, don't tell me. I don't even want to know."

"He's innocent," Petra said anyway. "He didn't know what he was getting himself into."

"And who ever does?"

The parlor was silent for several minutes, and Petra stared out the window at the seagulls circling the harbor, unwilling to force more information from Monty. He and his wife were already in danger. He owed them nothing.

"I have been up to the Sixth Rise headquarters, but not through the main entrance," Monty finally said. "There is another way in, one which I helped build, though I don't claim credit for the entire thing."

"And... And why didn't you tell us this before?" Petra asked in what she hoped was a respectful tone.

The inventor shrugged. "Cat's out of the frying pan

now. I had hoped you might solve your problem with the Guild face to face, instead of infiltrating them in a way that is *sure* to provoke them."

Seventeen

PETRA

"Can you slow down a bit?" Petra whispered to Evan. "This tunnel is obscenely low."

"That, or you're obscenely tall."

She snorted and bumped her shoulder into his as they pushed a small cart down a set of tracks. "Jealous?"

"Not really," he said easily, and she believed him. Most men were intimidated by her height even when they said they weren't.

"Here, let's stop for a bit," he said. "I think the lantern's about to fall over again."

She halted, not wanting to experience the total blackness of the tunnel like the last time the lamp had fallen over and extinguished. They had gotten the old-fashioned oil lamp, along with the cart, at the beginning of the tunnel entrance where Monty had told them they would find it, right on the Low Rise.

Apparently, Monty and a few other inventors had

helped create a network of tunnels throughout Harrowdel decades ago, one entrance on each rise, leading up to the main Guild headquarters. It was ludicrous, that the Guild had this much infrastructure hidden under the city. They had already passed by several other tunnels, no doubt the entrances from the other rises. By Petra's count, they were somehow up on the Fifth Rise already. She had no idea what time it was anymore, and she didn't want to ask Evan to check his pocket watch and know for sure how long they had been pushing this infernal cart.

While Evan fixed the lamp's position yet again, Petra peeled off her coat, careful of all the things she liked to keep in its pockets. After setting it on one of the seats of the cart, she leaned against the smooth tunnel wall, which was cool against her sweaty skin, her bare arms pressing against the stone.

Monty had said the cart normally ran by itself, but if it hadn't been used in a while, the charge would be dead. They didn't have time to recharge it down at the tunnel entrance, but they would want it to return once they found Jiordan and—hopefully—escaped with him. They could leave it to charge at the Guild headquarters while they went inside, Monty had told them.

Once they got in, well that was a whole 'nother issue entirely.

Six tracks met up at the end of the tunnel. The cart they pushed was on the one all the way to the right. Petra and Evan both slumped against the back of the cart after pushing it up to the post where it would charge, ready for their escape. There was a hiss as it connected to the post, then a buzz and a whir as it seemingly began to charge.

"Well, here we are," Evan said.

"Here we are," she agreed, closing her eyes to rest for a minute. For a split-second, she thought of the tea shop, wishing she were back there with Maisie, holed up in the kitchen together talking over nothing. She sighed. *Not there yet.*

"Now what?" Evan asked.

"Now we get Jiordan."

"I don't suppose you have a clue as to *how* we're going to go about doing that?"

Petra shrugged, opening one eye to peer at him in the near-dark tunnel. "You really don't like not having a plan, do you?"

"Hah!" he laughed. "I thought *you* were the one who needed a plan."

She flushed, not having realized he had known that about her.

He went on, "I can deal with a little improvisation; adventuring isn't all the exciting bits you read about in the papers."

"The good parts, you mean."

Evan snorted. "I happen to like planning. I wouldn't do this for a living if I didn't."

"All right, all right, I'm not one to talk," she said. "Maisie would say I didn't know how to scratch my nose without making a plan first. But I'm trying to learn to improvise."

"Well," Evan said, rubbing his hands together, "since we've just infiltrated the Guild of the Rose through a secret tunnel and are staring at their back door, are you ready to work on it a little more?"

"Yes, yes, yes. I can handle it. Let's just do it. Are you ready?" Petra rose and held out a hand to help Evan up.

"As much as I can be," he said, accepting it and letting his fingers linger in hers for a moment. "I do wish we had brought some of those little cakes from the shop and maybe a flask of tea or something."

Petra tsked. "I won't tell Maisie you like those store-bought cakes." Her own stomach growled at the thought. The cakes from Madam Angelford's *were* quite good, especially the almond ones, but she would never admit it to her sister either.

Then her heart grew heavy. She still had no idea where Maisie was. But maybe after they got Jiordan, they could start looking for their sister together.

"If Monty's right," Evan began, "this door should let out in the lowest level of the complex." He went over and leaned an ear against the nondescript door set in the black stone wall.

"Unless they built more after he worked for them, but it's a start." Petra came up behind him and motioned for him to step aside. She pulled out one pistol and pressed her back to the wall beside the door, then eased it open.

She could see an empty corridor, dimly lit and with the black and white checkered floor just like the brief glimpse they had gotten of the ground level. Red wallpaper and gold sconces graced the walls, but no windows, considering they were underground.

"It's quiet," she told Evan. "I don't see anyone."

"Let's stay together, shall we?"

Petra nodded, and eased the door open further. Slipping into the corridor, she glanced up and down it to be sure it was empty. She motioned for Evan to follow, and he shut the tunnel door behind him.

"This way?" Evan suggested, pointing to the right.

"Wait," Petra said. "I want to remember where this door is."

"Across from the painting of the white Frannish terrier, the frame chipped on the bottom right corner."

Petra looked at him in astonishment. He pointed to the opposite wall. There was indeed a hideous painting of a little white terrier sitting on a red velvet cushion. She looked closer and saw the chip on the frame. "How did you—"

He cocked his head. "I do this for a living, how many times do I have to tell you? Well, not all this illegal entering, but you know—"

They both froze, and Petra's heart seemed to skip a beat. Footsteps came from the left, along with the sound of clinking bottles.

Evan jerked his thumb to the right, and they both

darted down the corridor as quietly as they could. They rounded the corner and pressed their backs to the wall, listening. The footsteps were still coming this way. A door nearby was open a crack, and Evan peered inside. He waved to Petra, who followed him in.

It was just as dimly lit as the corridor outside, with a single gas lamp set in the wall in a modest gold sconce. It was a homely sort of room, full of old wooden shelves and tables each covered in an impressive display of glass bottles of all sizes and shapes, all with neat labels, filled with different colored liquids or powders. Petra stationed herself beside the door, which they had returned to its original cracked position.

The footsteps were still coming in this direction, so it *was* best that they had hidden. Petra didn't want to hide in this alchemyst's storage closet; she would rather confront whomever they encountered and demand they show them where Jiordan was being kept, but she didn't think Evan would like that plan.

But the footsteps were getting too close. Catching Evan's panicked look, she shrugged. Perhaps she would get to go with her plan after all. Evan hid behind the door, and they waited.

When the hooded man walked into the room carrying a simple wooden tray with two bottles on it, he nearly walked into Petra's pistol, pointed between his eyes.

The tray in his hands shook, the bottles rattling against each other. Then suddenly the bottles were careening toward the floor, and Petra spared a worried thought for what kind of alchemycal concoctions could be inside them, but it was too late. Her pistol hand didn't waver as she watched the tray and bottles fall out of the corner of her eye.

No sound of breaking glass met her ears though, and she spotted Evan straightening up with both bottles in his hands.

"Nice try," Evan said to the man. "Next time don't try 'accidentally' covering someone in chemicals until you're sure you're alone."

"I—I—didn't mean," the man stuttered.

"Sure, sure," Petra said. "Now get in here." She yanked the front of his scholarly robes, and pulled him into the room, closing the door all the way. His hood had fallen back when she yanked him in, and she took in his grey hair and familiar face as she grabbed the wooden tray out of his hands and threw it aside.

"Weston?" she cried, almost lowering her pistol. "How—why—*what?* You almost dumped chemicals on me!"

Her new tea server had the decency to look ashamed of himself as he bowed his head and clasped his hands before him. "I'm sorry, Miss Everturn. They're not harmful."

"The shop! Did you just abandon it to come here after spying on us?"

"What?" he replied. "No! No. It's—it's after closing Miss Everturn."

"Oh," Petra said, amazed at how long it had taken them to walk up the tunnel. "But still—you were spying on us!"

"Ah," he hedged, not refuting it. "I'm really, *truly* sorry for everything."

"You're about to be," she said, advancing on him with her pistol practically shoved up his nose. She grabbed the front of his robes and pressed him up against the back of the door.

"You worm your way into my family's tea shop just to spy on us? What for? Your Guild already had Jiordan."

Weston looked everywhere except the pistol and Petra's eyes. "I'm sorry," he said again. "But I'm so low in the ranks here, I *had* to do it. If I ever want to make apprentice even, I had to. Sir Anton said I was just to keep an eye on you and your sister, and report your whereabouts to him. I really do like serving tea," he added in a small voice.

"Well you won't be welcome back in Everturn's Finest Tea Shoppe as long as you live." Petra realized she was shaking, and she backed off, handing her pistol to Evan who dutifully kept it pointed at Weston's gut. She turned away for a second to gather her thoughts.

"You were reporting our whereabouts?"

He nodded.

"Then where is Maisie?"

"I—I don't know. I was training with you at the shop when she disappeared."

Oh, right. "Well, why were you spying on us then?"

"I don't know, I just did what I was told. Everyone's always said I would make a good actor," he mumbled.

Petra huffed. "You're pathetic," she said, all ire gone.

The older man cowered in the corner with his hands over his face.

"Maybe they're trying to find out where the Mirror is," Evan said quietly to Petra.

She bit the inside of her lip. That seemed about right. If Jiordan had had it on him, they would have taken it when they arrested him. But if he had hidden it, well, it would be best that it remained hidden. It might be the only reason they were going through all this business with Jiordan's trial, even if it was behind closed doors. She nodded at Evan.

"Right, then," she said, drawing her second pistol from inside her coat and pointing it at Weston. "You're going to bring us to Jiordan."

"I really don't know if he's down here," Weston warbled as they trudged down a dark corridor, lit only by the electric lantern in Petra's hand. "I've never seen him in person exactly."

They had taken a set of stairs down to another level, this one without the checkered floors and luxury wallpaper of the floors above. Petra knew it was because the Guild hadn't let their inventors and contractors help build this part of the complex. This had to be it. Where they kept prisoners, whether it was legal or not. She still wasn't sure if Anton was telling the truth about that.

"Yeah, sure," Petra said, holding the fancy electric lantern higher. Weston had taken it from the room with all the bottles before leading them down here, then cranked a gear on its side for a few minutes to charge it up. He walked in front, with both Evan and Petra's sights set on him. It was as dark as the tunnel had been. Anyone that was being kept down here was in complete darkness. It was no way to treat a person.

A clang up ahead made her hand jerk, throwing lantern light haphazardly against the walls.

"What was that?" she hissed.

"I don't know," Weston said, stopping. She nudged him forward with the mouth of her pistol, and he crept on, hands raised awkwardly.

"Petra," Evan said. "Look."

There on the right was a door—the first door they had seen yet—with bars at the top.

"You watch him," she whispered to Evan, who nodded, eyes trained on Weston.

Petra approached the door, lantern held aloft, pistol at the ready. She was tall enough to see through the bars at the top, into what was obviously a cell. It was empty.

She turned back to Evan and shook her head. "Let's keep going."

They checked four more cells. They were all empty. *How many cells do they need down here?* she wondered. *How many people have they held prisoner? This is so wrong.*

When she held the lantern up to the next bars, she gasped. Staring at her from across the cell was her brother.

Eighteen

PETRA

"Jiordan!" Petra cried. She turned and pressed the lantern into Evan's hands, then rushed back to the bars. "Quick, how do we get you out of there?"

Her brother stood up and stared at her, his mouth slightly open. He looked older, much older than the year or so it had been since she had seen him last. He had beard stubble from being locked up, and after spending so much time with Evan she didn't think it looked too strange on him. His normally tidy blonde hair was falling into his eyes, and his clothes were worn and ripped in more than a few places.

"Petra? Is that you?"

"Of course it's me! We've come to get you."

To her astonishment, he sat back down. He crossed his arms and squinted at her, shaking his head. "No thanks."

"What do you mean, *no thanks*? Do you have any idea how much trouble it's been trying to find you?"

He merely shrugged and leaned back against the wall, looking away.

Petra rattled the door, while Evan shushed her. "You get over here right now Jiordan Everturn, or so help me— I will come in there and knock your legs out from under you."

Jiordan sat up. "Petra? Is that really you?"

Petra exchanged a worried look with Evan. "What's wrong with him?" she whispered.

Finally, Jiordan bolted to the door. "I didn't think it was really you," he said in a rush, getting close and studying her face. "And Evan! I didn't see you there! The Guild has been trying all kinds of ways to trick me into telling them where the Mirror is. I thought they might have finally figured out how to make a dopple potion or something. But they couldn't possibly copy your personality, Petra." He grinned, new wrinkles around his eyes creasing.

Passing over the idea of a potion like that, Petra said, "How do we get you out of here? Are there keys somewhere?"

Jiordan shook his head. "I've no idea. Whenever they open the door, Anton is there, though. I suspect he has the keys."

"Anton?" Petra said. She turned to Weston. "Where is he?"

Weston's eyes grew wide in the lantern light. "I—I— don't know, perhaps up in his workshop, but I think he was readying for the gathering."

"Gathering?"

"Yes, for the autumn equinox tonight, the sun is crossing the celestial—"

"What kind of gathering is it?" Petra cut across him.

"Ah, it's somewhat of a Guild-wide meeting, all the Harrowdel chapter will be there."

Petra rolled her eyes. "Great. All the alchemysts are coming to the headquarters while we're stuck down here trying to get Jiordan out." She turned to Evan and hissed, "See? This is why I like solid plans."

He shrugged. "I thought you were working on your improvising?"

"*Working on it*," she muttered through gritted teeth. "Well? Where would we find Anton and his key?" she asked Weston.

But Evan spoke instead, "I don't know if confronting Anton for the keys is a good idea. Besides, we shouldn't go wandering around the complex if we don't have to, especially if there are going to be a lot of people gathering. And that Anton fellow seemed dangerous."

"I agree," Jiordan said. "He's got some nasty alchemycal tricks up his frivolous sleeves—and so do the rest of them."

Petra rattled the large padlock on the door and let out a frustrated breath. "Well, looks like we're going with plan B, then. Jiordan, step away from the door." She pointed her pistol at the lock. Weston covered his ears.

"Wait, no, Petra! How is this a good plan? It'll be too loud—" Evan protested.

"I don't care. We just need to make it back to the tunnel. It's not even that far. I think we can fight off a few wimpy alchemysts if they come looking." She threw a glance back at Weston, who backed away to the edge of the lantern's light, looking down.

Petra took Evan's hand and pulled him behind her as she pressed herself against the wall to avoid any ricochet. Then she raised her arm to the lock, and fired.

A sharp *clang* broke the dark silence as the bullet devastated the padlock, ripping it open. Petra held her breath for a moment, listening for any sound of alarm. There was none. She just hoped they were deep enough underground and far away from whatever gathering was going on.

She rushed over and ripped the broken lock off, yanking the door open.

Jiordan stepped out and pulled her into a hug. She closed her eyes for a moment, resting her chin on his shoulder. Tears threatened her eyes, but she dashed them away before they pulled apart.

"I thought you were d—I thought you weren't coming home. You have no idea what you've put Maisie and me through," she said, facing him now. "That trunk? Telling us you were dead? What were you thinking?"

Jiordan gave her a sheepish grin and shrugged. "It seemed like a good idea at the time; I needed help and had to get your attention. Well, where's Maisie?"

Petra looked down. "I don't know. She disappeared almost a week ago, looking for the Guild. They said they didn't have her, but we think it could have been the woman with the ruby eye who took her."

"Oh," Jiordan said, taking a steadying breath. "Well, you came this far finding me; I'm sure we'll find Maisie, together." He cleared his throat. "And Evan Rosslyn came to help, who'd have thought?"

Evan shifted the lantern to his pistol hand to shake with Jiordan.

"Wait—" Petra said, noting Evan's loose grip on the pistol. "Where's Weston?"

The three of them looked around the otherwise empty corridor. Petra snatched the lantern back from Evan, shining it up and down the hallway.

"Evan!" she hissed, rounding on him. "You were supposed to be watching him! Now he's run off to tell someone we've busted out Jiordan!"

"I think your pistol did that job for us," Evan retorted. "I told you not to shoot it. He probably ran off when you fired."

Petra took a breath to yell at him, but Jiordan put a hand on her arm.

"Look," he said sharply, pointing at the floor.

She lowered the lantern to reveal a dark stain on the stone floor, surrounded by shards of glass.

"Well that can't be good," Jiordan said. "You... didn't search him?"

Neither Petra nor Evan answered. Petra closed her eyes in a long blink, cursing herself. She was really bad at this whole flying-by-the-seat-of-her-trousers thing.

"Well, let's get away from it," Jiordan suggested. "Which way did you come from?"

"This way," Petra and Evan said, pointing in different directions.

Petra smirked. "I thought you were paying attention, Evan. We came from the right of the door."

"Well, we also came from the direction that had this weird sconce," Evan said, pointing to a wrought-iron hand holding an unlit candle.

Petra frowned, glancing up and down the hallway. "There's probably more than one sconce. We came from the right."

"Let's get away from this potion or elixir or whatever," Jiordan said, going with Petra and backing away from the stain on the floor. "He probably smashed it when you fired, so we've probably already breathed it in, but—"

"Come on, Evan, this way," Petra said, withdrawing down the corridor, practically skipping now that she had found Jiordan.

Evan glanced at the sconce and shook his head, reluctantly following. "Fine."

"So how did you find me?" Jiordan asked as they crept down the corridor. "The trunk?"

Petra scoffed. "In a roundabout way, I guess. It was stolen from us before we could figure out what it was, but the woman who stole it led us to believe the Guild of the Rose had something to do with it all."

"It was stolen?"

"Sorry. What was in there?"

"Nothing, actually. The clue was the top. I thought for sure you'd figure it out."

"You know I don't know anything about alchemy."

"It wasn't alchemy! It was from that story Father used to read us, the *Sapphire Lion*. It was one of my favorites, don't you remember?"

Petra thought about it for a moment, thinking back to the long night they had spent in their father's workshop studying the tracing of the tableau. "The blue lion," she muttered. "You idiot. How were we supposed to figure that out? And what would it have told us, anyway?"

"It was leading to a safe place where I left the Mirror. I didn't know I'd be separated from it at the time..."

Evan started chuckling. "I guess we should have checked the children's storybooks in your father's collection. What were we thinking?"

Petra started laughing too as they reached the corner and turned left.

"Weren't the stairs that way?" Evan asked.

Petra furrowed her eyebrows and glanced up and down the next corridor. "I thought..."

"Were you two even paying attention when you came to rescue me or—" Jiordan started.

"Of course!" Petra snapped. "But I thought it was this way!"

She shoved the lantern into Jiordan's hands and paced around the intersection of the two corridors.

"Maybe we should go back to the cell," Evan suggested quietly. "I told you I thought we came from the other direction."

"You shut your mouth Evan Rosslyn," Petra said. "You're the one who let Weston go, and let him drop some potion on us—"

"The potion," Jiordan said, snapping his fingers. "Perhaps it was one to invoke confusion, or something—"

Footsteps became clear from the direction of the cell. Jiordan quickly shut off the lantern, and the three of them ducked around the corner. Petra was closest to the corner, and she poked her head out to listen.

"It's at least two people," she guessed. "Should we just go this way?" she asked the others.

Jiordan shrugged. In the almost complete darkness he looked exhausted, the new wrinkles on his face and the stubble making him look almost like a stranger. "Let's just go this way," he agreed. "There's got to be a way out somewhere, even if we're going in the wrong direction."

Just then voices floated toward them in the darkness.

"They'll be trapped down this way, sir," Weston said. "Be careful up here, that's where the elixir is."

"I see it," a voice replied in clipped tones. "Don't want to get turned about, do I? I'm surprised you found me so quickly after inhaling it yourself."

"I've spent a lot of time down in the lower levels," Weston replied, not without a little complaint. "I know them well enough to navigate them backwards."

Petra turned to look at Jiordan and Evan.

Backwards. Everything was backwards.

Nineteen

PETRA

"Let's go," she said, not caring what direction they were heading anymore. Though she dearly wanted to confront Weston, whoever was with him could be even more dangerous. She just hoped it wasn't Anton.

"*Elixirs*," she muttered as she hustled quietly down the corridor in the dark, holding both Evan and Jiordan's hands. "That's just cheating."

Evan snorted and squeezed her hand.

"Don't think I'm done being mad at you for letting Weston escape and poison us," Petra whispered to him.

"Oh, please," Evan said. "You can't possibly blame me. I'm not exactly an expert at holding people at gunpoint."

"Oh yeah? What about the first night we met?"

"Yes, I'd like to know about that myself," Jiordan chimed in.

"Mind your own business, brother."

"This way," Evan said, pulling them to the left, "that

looks like some stairs—there's light somewhere above."

Without question they followed. They were already turned around and lost. How much worse could it get?

At the top of the long flight of stairs that must have spanned two floors, they stopped at a closed door, and Petra could smell fresh air. A soft glow of light radiated underneath the crack in the door. She took a deep breath, smelling trees and freshly cut grass, and could hear the tinkling of water.

"The garden?" she whispered.

"Could be," Evan said.

"Let's go then," Jiordan said, on edge.

Petra turned the handle and opened the door. The lantern light blinded her after her time in the dark, and she flung a hand across her eyes. Then she heard the door slam behind them. Slowly she blinked her eyes open.

"Well, here's our guests," a voice came from amidst the blinding sea of lantern light.

Sir Anton Georgoff stepped forward, his scholarly red robes fluttering across the neatly-cropped grass. A teenaged boy stood by his side, dutifully holding a lantern on a pole.

Behind them stood more than a dozen robed men and women, all holding lanterns of their own. There were tables, chairs, and electric bauble lights strung about the garden behind them, set up to celebrate the equinox, it appeared.

Simultaneously Jiordan and Evan tried to push Petra behind them, but she stood her ground, anchored between the two of them. She and Evan still had pistols. What could these alchemysts do to them? She raised hers now, sighting it at Anton's middle.

Madam Malavia, the woman present on their first trip to the Guild, stepped up beside Anton, showing no fear at the pistol Evan was pointing at her torso. In fact, she clasped her hands behind her back, as if showing off a greater target. She was wearing another one of those tiny hats perched on her white hair, a black and red cap with flowers springing off the brim to match her robes. Petra scowled.

"Please let us go," Petra said. "Jiordan doesn't have the Mirror, and he didn't know it was used to kill people when he found it."

Anton shook his head. "But that doesn't negate the fact that he stole it from the Guild. He is awaiting trial."

"Then I'll bring him to the magistrate's dungeons," Petra said, unsure if she really would. She couldn't let the Guild keep him. He wouldn't get a fair trial. Maybe they could all leave Harrowdel together, leave Adonia and go to Rancozzi or Frannia or somewhere. But that would mean leaving the tea shop.

"And then they would give you a cell right next to his," Anton said. "For helping a criminal escape in the first place."

Petra started shaking. If that were true, she would never find Maisie. "Look, he's not a criminal—"

"Petra, stop," Jiordan said, pulling her back a little.

She glanced at him, disbelieving. "What—?"

"I took the Mirror," he said. Whispers broke out in the crowd behind Anton. "You've already heard me say that," he said louder. "I'm not trying to deny that."

"But we can still try to get you out of here," Petra insisted.

Jiordan shook his head. "You can't wind up in a cell, Petra. And if you shoot our way out of here, the same thing will happen. You need to find Maisie. I'm not worth that."

Petra's eyes stung. "Stop it," she said, her voice cracking. She raised her pistol so it was pointing at Anton's smug face. His thick eyebrows cast in lantern light left horn-like shadows on his forehead.

"Lower your weapons," Anton said, "return Mr. Everturn to us, and you may go. I know family ties run deep, and I understand the lengths we take for our loved ones."

Madam Malavia glowered at Anton.

From Petra's other side, Evan put a gentle hand on her shoulder. "Maybe we should do what he says."

A silent tear slid down Petra's cheek, and she lowered her shaking pistol. *But we found him. I can't give him up.*

Anton nodded to someone they couldn't see, and two red-robed alchemysts emerged from the crowd, one carrying a delicate golden chain with triangular points at either end. They wove the chain around Jiordan's wrists, and Petra couldn't be sure, but she thought she saw the end points slither together, wrapping tightly around each other in a knot.

They pulled Jiordan away from Petra and Evan, who still had their backs to the dungeon door. Everyone in the crowd seemed to be pulling away, forming an arch around where Petra and Evan stood. She watched them pull her brother to stand beside Anton, who turned to address him.

"Now, Mr. Everturn, would you please tell me where the Mirror is."

"What? No, I told you—I'm not going to—"

"Please." Anton held up a small vial, its contents twinkling in the lantern light. It looked like some kind of bright pink powder. Anton glanced at Petra, and his meaning became clear.

"No! Don't hurt them!" Jiordan cried, struggling against his golden chains and captors. He fell to his knees, the two alchemysts holding him tightly around the arms.

Petra stood frozen beside Evan. No doubt that powder wasn't as innocuous as the elixir that turned them about. It could be anything. One of a thousand elixirs from that room they met Weston in.

Somehow her hand found its way into Evan's. They stared down Anton and his vial, and Petra wondered if this Mirror was really worth it.

She knew Jiordan was worth it, and that was something. Family was everything. She squared her shoulders and looked Anton in the eye, not bothering to raise her pistol. Surely he had calculated for that, and surely it would be useless against this.

It seemed like time froze around her. Evan's hand was

warm in hers, and she breathed in and out, relishing the cool night air in her lungs.

"No—wait!" Jiordan called, just as Anton tossed the vial at their feet.

At first nothing happened. Petra was still frozen in shock as whatever powder in the vial swirled in the air around them. But then she realized she was frozen from more than just shock. She couldn't move.

She could feel her hand in Evan's but couldn't pull it away. Her feet were stuck to the ground, but somehow her eyes could move, and undoubtedly her lungs. She watched Jiordan's look of horror as he realized what had happened.

"Petra, no!" he cried, yanking at his golden chains again. "No! She did nothing wrong! Release them!" he demanded, turning on Anton.

Another alchemyst strode up to Evan and Petra and yanked the pistols out of their hands, throwing them to the ground. Petra didn't feel the weapon being pulled from her fingers in the slightest. Had she lost sensation forever?

"I'll release them as soon as you tell me where the Mirror is. But if you don't, we might have some new statues in our garden." He chuckled.

Petra's eyes bulged. She couldn't look down; was she turning to stone? Would she become yet another strange statue in the Guild's garden forever?

"It would improve the place, wouldn't it?" a woman's voice called.

Madam Malavia let out a gasp, clutching her lace sleeves to herself.

The ruby-eyed witch stepped out from behind the shadow of a tree, followed by her grey-haired goon, who was nodding. He had a black eye, and his elegant clothes were a bit dusty. The woman's scarlet cloak looked somewhat rumpled, though her chestnut curls were immaculate, spilling over her shoulders. The ruby protruding from her eye socket glinted maliciously in the lantern-lit garden. Petra felt a strange sensation inside her body, what might have been a shudder, if she could feel anything.

The crowd drew back from the woman as she swept into the clearing. She put her hands on her hips. "Ah, the Everturns, always turning up in the most unexpected places. Or most of you, anyway." A coy smile rose to her lips.

"What did you do with Maisie?" Jiordan demanded.

"Me? Nothing at all. Now, I'm here for my Mirror. I know she brought it to you."

Both Jiordan and Anton gazed questioningly at Petra. Anton looked like he was about to speak when Madam Malavia interrupted.

"Leave this place, Tria," she said, her round spectacles flashing in the lantern light, her tiny hat shaking with her rage. "You've been cast out of the Guild. And your Mirror will never be returned to you."

The man with Tria crossed his arms tightly about himself. "But—"

"I don't want to hear you speak, Phillip. Get out of here, the both of you."

"I will have what is mine," Tria demanded, stalking forward.

"Never," Anton chimed in. "The Mirror is evil, and we would never give it back to you."

Tria laughed. "Evil? Evil? What does good and evil have to do with *discovery?* With *knowledge?* And where did you ever come to that conclusion about the Mirror anyway? From her?" she pointed at Madam Malavia. "She was merely jealous that I took Phillip from her, that I took her never-ending source of gold from her!"

Never-ending gold? Petra thought, then looked closer at the quality of the man's clothes. His shoes likely cost more than what it took to run the tea shop for a whole year. She had heard stories of alchemysts making gold, but hadn't thought any of it was real. Well, she knew better than to discard those kinds of tales anymore.

Madam Malavia chortled. "Yes, my dear, as you can see, I'm as poor as a pauper since my son left to run off with you. I have no need of more *gold*, Tria. What I wanted was my son."

"So you lied to the Guild about the Mirror!" Tria said, raising a maligning finger. "Ruining me and my work!"

"Of course not. It's a highly dangerous object that will end the life of anyone who touches it."

Petra's eyes were starting to water. She couldn't blink, and her gaze flickering back and forth between the two women was somehow exhausting. She wished she could look at Evan, just to look into his eyes again. See his silly beard and the roguish emerald in his ear. She didn't care that he was an adventurer. He was brave. And selfless. And kind.

While Madam Malavia and Tria shouted accusations at each other, Anton circled around the clearing toward Petra and Evan. Jiordan remained kneeling in his chains across from them.

"The Mirror," Anton insisted. "Do you have it?"

Petra just stared at him.

"Ah, yes. Look to the right if you have it, and all of this will be forgiven."

Petra kept staring straight ahead.

"Telling the truth now will give me enough time to administer the antidote elixir to the stoneseep powder."

She wanted to roll her eyes, or close them—or better yet, grab her pistol and shoot the infuriating man in the gut.

"Very well. I thought you might have it after what Tria said..." he trailed off.

What Tria had said. *I know she brought it to you.* She. Could she mean—?

Just then a string of bauble lights above popped and went out. The men and women gathered gasped and shrunk further into the darkness of the garden.

Standing on a nearby fountain ledge was Maisie, holding a crowbar and wearing a sailor's uniform.

Twenty

PETRA

"Let them go!" Maisie called, pointing her crowbar at Petra, Evan, and Jiordan.

Petra couldn't *believe* Maisie was here. Where had she even been? It was almost a whole week since she had disappeared, and now she was here in the Guild's garden?

Jiordan turned to Maisie with a mix of joy and terror on his face. "Maisie, you're all right," he choked. "Get out of the garden while you can!"

"I'm not going anywhere," Maisie said, addressing Anton and Tria, the two standing exposed in the open clearing. "It's been a long trip since I left home, and I'm not leaving without my brother and sister, and that one too," she added, pointing at Evan.

Anton stepped closer to Maisie. "My dear," he said tiredly, "I cannot allow Mr. Everturn to leave, as I have already explained to these two here. He has broken the law and stolen a dangerous artifact."

"Dangerous?" Maisie repeated. "You mean this?" She pulled a black velvet case out of a leather satchel, about the size of a book.

It felt as if Petra's heart stopped beating. Maisie didn't know. She didn't know the Mirror killed people.

Or did it?

Petra had no idea who was telling the truth anymore. It was Madam Malavia's word or Tria's. And she didn't trust either of them. But she couldn't believe Maisie would bring the Mirror here of all places.

And neither could Jiordan. He groaned, his head sinking toward the ground. "Maisie, no, you shouldn't have brought it!"

Don't touch the Mirror, Maisie, Petra thought, trying to will her thoughts to cross the distance between them. *Just don't touch it.*

Petra heard a rustle behind her. She couldn't turn to look, of course, and fear slithered up her spine at the thought of whoever might be creeping up behind them.

"It's me," a familiar voice said, but she couldn't place it. "Here, just stand still—" a strangled sound like a snort emerged from Petra somehow "—sorry, bad choice of words. I've got the powder to reverse it."

She smelled something like lavender, and a terrible tingling came over her, like the feeling after a leg has fallen asleep and is waking back up. But in every part of her body.

"Don't move yet, it's going to hurt. And... you might not want them to know you're free."

She turned her neck ever so slightly to the right—and felt like she broke every tendon in the process—but she spotted their rescuer. It was Weston.

"You—"

"Shh! If you come back through this door, I can guide you through the halls and to the exit tunnel. I'm really sorry Ms. Everturn. I didn't know Anton would do that to you, all over some artifact."

She turned to look at Evan finally, who appeared to be in about as much pain as she. Millions of prickles shuddered over her as she made the slightest movement. She caught his amber-colored eyes and the corners of her lips automatically turned up in a smile. He squeezed her hand, and though it hurt through the prickly feeling, it was good to feel the sensation of his hand in hers again.

Not wanting to go to all the trouble of shrugging, she mouthed, "Should we go?"

He grimaced.

"Step back," Maisie called, and Petra turned back to watch her reckless sister, waving the Mirror above her head. "I won't give this to anyone unless you release all of them."

"Don't give it to them!" Jiordan cried.

Petra agreed. None of these people deserved to have it, whether it killed people or not.

"Give it to me," Anton said. "It belongs to the Guild of the Rose to be protected, not to this heretic," he pointed at Tria.

"Liar!" Tria shot. "It is mine," she pleaded with Maisie.

"I know I wronged you, more than once, but it's my creation. I just wanted it back. Anton took it from me under false pretenses, and shamed me out of the Guild because of it. Your brother took it from where they had safeguarded it, and I just want to get it back!"

Petra could feel Weston's presence behind her as he shifted his feet, perhaps as eager to get out of here as they were. Sure, she and Evan could probably slip out this door unnoticed, but she couldn't just leave Jiordan and Maisie in the middle of all this.

She began stealthily slipping her hands in her pockets, looking for something—anything that could help. Of course, her pistols lay on the ground right in front of them, but she was sure someone would notice her bending down to get one—that is, if she could even withstand the hot needle sensation that shot through her any time she moved a muscle.

However, slowly moving one hand at a time to each pocket was somewhat manageable. She gasped when her hand wrapped around a spherical metal object.

At that moment, Maisie jumped down from the fountain and headed over to where Petra and Evan stood, not so frozen anymore. Petra wanted to hug her, and smack her head all at the same time, but she didn't dare move, now that Tria and Anton's attention had been drawn their way.

Maisie looked up at Petra and hissed, "Don't worry, I have a plan."

Twenty-One

MAISIE

With the ruby-eyed witch's disturbing gaze on her, Maisie put the velvet box containing the Mirror back in her satchel.

"I'm sorry it took so long to get here," Maisie said to the men and women gathered in front of her. The man who stood at the center, Sir Anton Georgoff—according to her information from Captain Ardmore—glowered at her.

"But I had to take a slight detour in the port after arriving from Amaryllia, where that woman was so kind to set me on my journey," she pointed at Tria with her crowbar. Elijah had let her take it, along with her new outfit and satchel.

She had also gained a better understanding of the Order of Branwen from Captain Ardmore on their hasty way back to Harrowdel.

After a quick trip to see a fellow member of the Order

in the port once they had docked, Maisie had what she needed to free Jiordan. She just hoped it would work.

No one on the *Scarborough* had been willing to part with any guns, but she had come this far without one; she could manage with cold hard iron.

"I'll be taking my brother now," Maisie said to the alchemysts.

"Give *me* the Mirror," Tria called. "We both want nothing to do with the Guild; why not give it back to me?"

Maisie shook her head. "I don't know if any of you deserve it, but I won't be giving it up until we're safe."

Tria whispered something to Captain Phillip, who plunged his hand inside his coat.

Before Maisie knew what was happening, she was flung to the ground, and the sound of a gunshot echoed in her ears.

She lay on the ground, her ears ringing. Her crowbar had fallen out of her hand, so she clutched the satchel to her chest with both hands, guarding the Mirror.

Then a sob met her ears.

"Evan!" Petra cried.

Petra crouched on the ground, evidently having pushed Maisie out of the way. Evan had taken the bullet instead. Somehow, both of them had gotten free of whatever strange alchemy had frozen them.

"Evan, no," Maisie said, crawling over to him, still clutching the satchel with one hand, and now fumbling in the grass for her crowbar. Then she spotted a pistol laying there instead. "Even better!" she muttered and snatched it up.

"Give me that," Petra growled, yanking the pistol out of Maisie's hand and aiming it at Phillip.

"No!" the old woman with the spectacles cried. "Phillip!"

The gun went off like a cannon in the spacious garden, and Phillip went down like a stone.

"No, no, my son!" the old woman cried, shoving Anton aside and rushing over to Phillip. Her hands came away red after touching his shoulder.

Maisie's stomach squirmed. Phillip's shot had been meant for her, but now both Evan and Phillip lay in the grass as if dead.

Petra sunk back down to cradle Evan's head in her lap, murmuring softly to him. The sight of her sister looking so tender toward anyone—especially Evan—shocked her.

She blinked tears from her eyes she hadn't even known were there, and stood straight up. She yanked out the Mirror again, this time flipping open the black velvet case.

"This ends now!" she called. "You let us all free, or I break it!" She bent down and snatched up her crowbar from the grass.

Anton, Tria, and Jiordan all cried, "No!"

"Do it!" called the old woman laying over Phillip. "Break the awful thing. Look what it did to my Phillip! Look what its mere existence can do! It's evil. It kills people."

"It is not evil," Tria said hotly. "It is a monumental discovery! It can transmit matter through space, the first of its kind!"

Maisie flicked her gaze between the two women, then looked to Petra on the ground with Evan, whose eyes were closed.

With tears carving tracks down her cheek, Petra raised her head and said, "Do it."

Without any further thought, Maisie swung the crowbar at the Mirror in her left hand, smashing it against the velvet box backing. The sound of tinkling glass was lost among the shrieks of Tria, and the shouts of indignation from Anton and Jiordan.

Maisie looked down at the ground to see the red shards among the close-cropped grass, and took a step away from them. She met Petra's gaze and nodded.

Tria sunk into the grass staring at the spot where the broken shards lay. "How could you? How *could* you? Do you have any idea how long I worked... It took ages to get the metals right..." she trailed off as if to herself.

Maisie looked away from her in disgust. She had shone more emotion over a piece of broken glass than she had toward her companion Phillip laying quite possibly dead on the ground beside her.

"Why?" Anton asked, pained.

Petra spoke before Maisie could say anything. "Neither of them was telling the truth," she said, nodding at Tria and Phillip's mother. She then pulled a gold chain from one of her coat pockets, with a golden sphere swinging from it.

Immediately Maisie understood. The Amaryllian

truth amulet from their father's workshop. She was shocked Petra trusted it, not knowing the science behind it and all.

But after everything Maisie had been through, she herself was beginning to realize there was more to the world than just the science of things.

There was mystery in the world. And magic. Even if it didn't appear that way at first.

Anton seemed to know what the amulet was as well, because he nodded and brought a hand to his chin in thought. He whispered something to the boy standing next to him, holding a lantern. The boy withdrew and seemed to gather the crowd of alchemysts with him. Their lanterns retreated further into the creepy garden, lit with its bauble lights strung between trees, casting shadows on the strange statues and fountains. What looked like an interrupted party was now over.

Maisie bent down beside Petra. Evan's eyes were open again. "Evan, are you all right?"

"I've been better," he replied jerkily.

Maisie's gaze was drawn to a dark spot of red on his ribs, mere inches away from his heart. His coat had been ripped by the bullet revealing the bloody skin, but it looked like it only just grazed the side of his torso.

"Thank goodness you're all right," Maisie gushed. "I didn't know you two could even move! And Petra, you saved me!"

Petra gave her a weary smile. "Our new tea server, Weston got us free."

Maisie furrowed her eyebrows.

"I'll tell you about it later."

Maisie suddenly became aware of Anton, his lantern on the ground, casting dramatic shadows on him. She looked over to see Phillip's mother weeping over the prone captain, but the man's hand reached up to pat her back. So he was all right, too. Tria held a similar vigil over the broken shards of glass, as she ran her hands through the grass around them.

"I think we'll be taking Jiordan now," Maisie said to Anton, trying to keep her voice from shaking.

Anton let out an exasperated sigh. "How many times do I have to tell you people? Mr. Everturn broke the law, regardless of the fact that the Mirror was here and is now destroyed. The notarized transcription of his confession will be here any day now, and then we can hold his trial."

"You can't be serious," Petra said. She sounded like she had a head cold.

"This transcription?" Maisie inquired, pulling a bundle of papers from her satchel, a yellow wax seal on the outside.

Anton gaped at her. "You—how dare you? Those are official transcripts from the Amaryllian notary!"

"No, they're not. They're fakes you commissioned from a forger in Amaryllia. They're not from the notary at all. This whole thing is illegal. The confession, holding Jiordan, the closed-door trial. It's not in the magistrate's records at all is it?"

"But—but how would you even know—How did you

get—"

"Because I have some new friends I can trust—and they're everywhere. My new friends had acquired some illegal documents from a merchant," Maisie said. "And I went to retrieve them right after I docked. I think the Harrowdel Gazette—or better yet, the magistrate himself—would love to see some 'official transcripts' that have a forger's receipt with them, addressed to you, wouldn't you say?"

Anton couldn't seem to speak, his face growing as red as his robes.

Maisie continued, waving the papers. "So I think you're going to let Jiordan go—the item he may or may not have stolen is here, isn't it? It's in the grounds of the Guild. And whether or not it does what you say it did, well that's up for debate. Would you like to bring that question to the magistrate too?"

Mouth open in horror, Anton sputtered, "Get—fine! Get out of here! All of you!"

"With pleasure," Jiordan said, holding out his chained wrists. Anton did something with the ends of the chains, and they slithered right off and fell to the ground.

Petra and Jiordan lifted Evan and brought him to the door behind them, hidden in the ivy.

Maisie took one look at Tria weeping on the ground and turned her back on the garden.

Twenty-Two

MAISIE

Maisie and Petra walked on either side of the two-seat cart headed for the First Rise. Petra had gotten two fancy electric lanterns from the gentleman who had brought them to the tunnel—Weston, their tea server, apparently. Maisie was glad Evan could sit in the cart, with Jiordan to keep him from falling out. Jiordan didn't much look up for a long walk himself, with the dark circles under his eyes and worn and torn clothes probably hiding bruises or worse. Maisie hadn't wanted to help carry either of them all the way back to the tea shop.

The cart could go much faster, they had learned, but Evan said the speed made him woozy. So they had spent the time talking as the cart rolled easily down the tracks, watching as other tunnels split off to lead to the other rises.

Maisie had already recounted her adventures aboard the *Scarborough*, and her encounter with Sterling and the

Order of Branwen in Amaryllia. Petra and Evan were impressed to hear about Maisie's discovery that not only was Captain Ardmore a member of the Order, but so were their parents.

Jiordan had been surprisingly quiet, hardly even commenting when Maisie told them how she and Elijah figured out the clue of the Sapphire Lion.

It had grown quiet. The only sounds were their footsteps and the rolling of the covered metal wheels on the sleek cart.

"So, how's the tea shop?" Maisie asked to break the silence.

"It's fine," Petra said. "But I want to hear from you, Jiordan. What happened, what was all this for? Evan's been shot, Maisie was kidnapped and went to another country, and you haven't said a word. You're not upset about the Mirror are you?"

Maisie looked at her older brother in the lamp light. His eyes were closed, and he had a hand to his forehead.

Finally, he said, "It was stupid to take the Mirror."

"No kidding," Petra said.

"I had no idea the Guild of the Rose was behind it, or that there was a schism between them and its creator. I had only heard what everyone else had—what it could do."

"Sounds like you need to learn to do more research," Petra said, and Maisie could have sworn she winked at Evan.

"Yes, that's fair," Jiordan said. "I shouldn't have acted not knowing who was behind the Mirror and what the consequences would be."

"But would it really have been worth it?" Maisie asked. "Why did you want it in the first place? You get by just fine traveling the normal way."

Jiordan hesitated.

"Come on," Maisie said. "We just rescued you from a bunch of crooked alchemysts; you have to tell us."

He sighed. "I wanted to see if I could track down more about Father and Mother's disappearance in Scitica."

Maisie inhaled sharply. "Why? Do you know something?"

He shook his head. "No, only what we were all told. But with the Mirror and its supposed powers, I could travel to the deepest reaches of the Scitican mountains, and the highest points, without any of the dangers of an expedition. I could actually go and *look* for more clues, instead of just doing nothing about it for all these years."

"Oh," Maisie said, and her lantern dropped a little. They walked on in silence for a few moments, Maisie's thoughts churning. "Well, you know, brother, some of us have no intention of going off on expeditions, or stealing dangerous artifacts to get answers. Some of us just stay home, and honor their memory by living our daily lives like they would want us to, and carrying on their values."

She bit her lip, unable to speak anymore. She didn't want to be mad at Jiordan after just having rescued him, but to say they were doing *nothing*...

Petra added, "It's not doing *nothing*, Jiordan. It's called living."

Jiordan didn't say anything for a long time.

Finally, they reached the tunnel for the First Rise, and Maisie remembered something. "But did the Mirror even do what any of them said it did?" She looked at Petra.

"Like I said, both Madam Malavia and Tria were lying. And Madam Malavia said it was evil and killed people, so that's not true. And Tria said…"

"That it transmitted matter across space," Evan chimed in.

"Right," Petra said. "So apparently it didn't do that either."

"The ruby-eyed witch really seemed convinced though," Maisie said.

"Well, we all convince ourselves things can be true when they really aren't," Jiordan said quietly.

Maisie smiled and put a hand on her brother's shoulder.

"Don't feel bad, Jiordan," Evan said in a loud whisper. "I wanted the Mirror, too, you just got there before me."

"Well why did you really want it?" Jiordan asked gruffly.

"Me? I just wanted to travel the world."

Epilogue

PETRA

"Hurry up with those scones, would you?" Petra called into the kitchen. She dared not go in; there was a cloud of flour permeating the air, and the smell of something possibly burning. The clatter of a bowl and a yelp came from Maisie as a reply.

Petra hustled to get behind the tea counter, putting away the tins left out from last night's late tea-drinking after they had left the tunnel.

It was almost eight o'clock. They had six reservations at opening, and no one had even put any water on to boil yet.

"Jiordan!" Petra went over to the basement workshop door and stuck her head in the stairwell. "Get up here! I thought you were going to put the water on before we opened?"

"I will, I will," Jiordan called, coming to the bottom of the spiral staircase, a journal in his hand. He looked at his pocket watch and balked. "Sorry, sis, is it that time already?"

Petra huffed and turned away, going behind the counter to fill five kettles with fresh water and place them on the different burners. She knew Mr. Ingston would be drinking his usual Brass Breakfast tea, and he always liked it piping hot; it would take at least five minutes for it to get to the right temperature. She looked at the giant clock on the wall across from her, a beautiful gilded timepiece with birds and flowers carved in the frame. There might be enough time.

Jiordan stomped up the stairs and closed the workshop door, just as Maisie flew in with a tray of fresh pecan scones.

"Here," Maisie said, handing the tray to Jiordan. "Put those on the three-tiered display. No—not that one! The gold tray is for petit-fours. The silver one is for scones."

Jiordan chuckled. "You know, I did run the tea shop for a few years before you two."

"Well, get used to doing it our way, brother," Petra said, taking a small brass key out of her pocket and unlocking the enormous black and gilt cash register to double-check its contents. "We outnumber you. And if Maisie says the scones go on the silver one, then you better listen to her."

He chuckled again and began stacking the scones on the tiered tray in the bright window.

The bell above the door jingled and Petra looked up from the register in panic, but it was just Evan. He was holding himself stiffly, she knew because of the large bandage wrapping around his torso. They had looked at it last night as soon as they got back to the shop; the bullet had gone through and nicked a rib, but not broken it. She smiled at him, then cocked her head, noticing someone coming in behind him.

"Monty?" she asked in disbelief. She had thought he would have been long gone from Harrowdel by now with his wife.

Montgomery Hartford pushed his black spectacles higher up on his nose and removed his black top hat upon entering. He drew a deep breath and smiled. "Ah, what a wonderful smell this place always has. Reminds me of all the times I came to visit your father back in the days before I had my own shop."

Petra smiled sadly. Maisie came back out of the kitchen with a tray of petit-fours, and she placed them on the tea counter, studying the newcomer.

"This is the inventor we told you about," Petra told her. "He helped us—"

"No need to go into detail, my dear," Monty said, running his hands around the rim of his hat in front of him. "Mr. Rosslyn here informs me that our mutual friends no longer have issue with Jiordan or any doings related to him—I've already been back to my shop. The damage was superficial. Nothing lost, nothing broken, well except a few plant pots."

"Oh, thank goodness," Petra said, leaning across the counter to grab a purple petit-fours off the tray. She closed her eyes in bliss. "Maisie, we missed your baking," she said, her mouth full.

Maisie laughed and the sound wove through the morning-bright shop like the best-smelling tea in the world. "Well I haven't gone rusty, though I shudder to think what you might say about the tasteless biscuits they made me make on the *Scarborough*. They never did let me use any of their sugar. Oh! That reminds me. Elijah should be coming by today with his father. I owe them some *real* pastries. I'm going to make Elijah a dozen cinnamon buns. Maybe two."

"Monty, let me get you some tea," Petra offered.

"Oh sure, whatever you have brewing. It smells wonderful. I'll sit and stay a while. Adora is out buying new plants. She'll find me here when she's done—it might take a while." He carefully ambled off to the corner chair, a wingback upholstered in red and gold, and settled in.

"Jiordan, go get the napkins from the linen drawer," Petra said, "and bring Monty a cup of the Hazelnut I've got on the back counter." He nodded and disappeared.

Maisie took the plate of petit fours over to the window and started arranging them on the gold tray, humming a tune.

"Any of that Hazelnut tea for me?" Evan asked Petra across the counter.

"Of course," Petra said. "You can have all the Hazelnut tea you like, after I got you shot."

He smiled as she slid a steaming hot cup toward him. "It wasn't your fault at all. Who knows where the bullet could have struck Maisie? It only grazed me; I'm fine."

"If you say so. Look, I wanted to ask you something." She turned away from him and poured her own cup of tea, trying to find the right words. She wrapped her hands around the thick mug with roses painted on it that had been her mothers, and turned back to him.

"I... like you Evan Rosslyn. But my home is here, in Harrowdel, at the tea shop. I know you want to explore the world, but—"

He leaned across the tea counter and wrapped his hands around hers, the steam from the cup rising between their faces. "I'll stay."

"For now," she said. "I'm a realist Evan; you explorers don't stay put for long." And she was all right with that. After their adventure together, she realized there was nothing wrong with being happy in the moment. Even if she knew the moment might not last, at least it would make her happy for a time.

"Yes, for now," he agreed. "But I'd like to stay in Harrowdel, maybe get some more permanent accommodations up here on the First Rise. I think there's a lot in this city I haven't seen, and I want to see it with you."

Her face warmed, from more than just the rising steam. He lifted one hand and touched her chin, gently lifting up her face to kiss her on the lips. His beard brushed her cheek and she pulled away smiling.

"You're something else, Evan Rosslyn."

"Well I'd like to be *your* something else, if you'll have

me."

"I suppose," she said, and leaned forward to kiss him once more, not caring that Maisie had just walked by with her empty pastry tray. "Just don't do anything to force me to rescue you like my idiot brother did, all right?"

"I promise."

She chuckled, and the bell above the door rang. But it wasn't the first customer of the day, it was Weston.

"I'm sorry, Miss Everturn," he said, pulling off his bowler cap and holding it tentatively over his heart, as if it might protect him. "I didn't mean to cut it so close to opening."

Petra opened her mouth to speak, then closed it. "Y-You—" she sputtered. "Just what do you think—"

"Please listen to me," he said, edging toward the counter. "I put in my resignation at the Guild. I had no idea they would imprison someone illegally—and after they used my stoneseep powder on you, well, I never want anything to do with them."

Petra looked at Evan, who merely shrugged. She noticed the slight wince of pain at the motion, and made a note to make an appointment with their doctor for him, whether he wanted to go or not.

"Your powder?" she said with acid.

"Um, yes, I do all the—I did all the elixir prep, ma'am, as one of the low-ranking initiates. And for him to use it on you was just wrong. I had no idea my work would be put to use like that. It was intended for dangerous animals when I invented it."

Petra slammed the cash register drawer shut. "But you had no problem spying on us before that."

"That—that was when I thought they were acting legally! That your brother was guilty and being processed by the letter of the law! Please, I never meant you any harm. Let me make it up to you. Keep me on as a server. At least until you hire someone to replace me."

She looked up at the clock. "Very well. You do have a knack for it. But if I so much as suspect a whiff of untruth about your story, I'll truss you up in front of the magistrate's office, understand?"

Weston nodded, and hurried behind the tea counter to exchange his hat for an apron.

"I'm impressed," Evan said. "I thought you'd grab the shotgun and run him out of here."

"Well, someone once told me I shouldn't solve everything with bullets; I'm trying it out. Besides, if we— well, who am I kidding, if *Jiordan* ever gets in trouble with the Guild again, we'll have Weston in our corner."

Evan grinned and took a long draft of his tea. "I like it. Smart *and* cunning."

Petra took up her mug and finished it off, noticing Evan was still watching her.

"Well, Miss Everturn? Is everything how you want it?"

"It is," she grinned.

The bell rang over the door, and the day began.

The End

Also by Liz Delton

Everturn Chronicles
The Alchemyst's Mirror

The Arcera Trilogy
Meadowcity
The Fifth City
A Rift Between Cities
Sylvia in the Wilds (A Short Story)

The Realm of Camellia Series
The Starless Girl
The Storm King
The Gray Mage
The Rogue Shadow

The Clockwork Ice Dragon:
A Steampunk Christmas Novella

About the Author

Liz Delton writes and lives in New England, with her husband and sons. She studied Theater Management at the University of the Arts in Philly, always having enjoyed the backstage life of storytelling.

She reads and writes fantasy, especially the kind with alternate worlds. World-building is her favorite part of writing, and she is always dreaming up new fantastic places.

She loves drinking tea and traveling. When she's not writing you can find her hands full with one of her many craft projects.

Visit her website at **LizDelton.com**

Made in the USA
Middletown, DE
18 October 2022

12821781R00132